I0654135

Chapter 1

"Changing the name of the city was a great idea." Said *Discerner.*

"Yes, indeed." Agreed Judge. "Can you imagine keeping the original name of the city? I mean, who names a city *Slattersville?* We would still be carrying that *wasteful* name "*slatters*". I like the word play you used! *Awkward!*" They both laughed.

When the laughter died away, a grave yet resolute look fell over both their faces, and for a moment there was silence.

"It is time to go and search for the old book. We need to find out what is in it." Declared Discerner.

Nede Land 3: © 2020 by Yeral E. Ogando
The Hero Within - Volume Five
Publisher: Christian Translation LLC
Printed in the USA

This is a work of fiction. Names, characters, dialogue, places, and incidents are either a product of the author's imagination and are used fictitiously. Character's opinions are not necessarily the same as the authors. Any resemblance to persons living or dead is purely coincidental; they are not to be interpreted as real people or events.

ISBN 13: 978-1-946249-21-0

1. Series Fiction 2. Spiritual Warfare 3. Christian Fiction.

DEDICATION:

This book is dedicated to the unique and ever-lasting person who has always been there for me, no matter how stubborn I am:

GOD

I also want to dedicate this work to YOU (Rey Luis and Seferina), my beloved grandparents because without you, I would not be here. May you rest in peace with our Lord Jesus Christ in heaven! You were, and shall always remain, the best part of me.

I WILL ALWAYS LOVE YOU.

Always.

ACKNOWLEDGMENTS:

Thanks to God for allowing my dream to come true, and for giving me strength when I felt like giving up.

Had it not been for the support that I have received along the way from these incredible and amazing people, I would not be where I am today.

Thanks to my editor, Lucas Walsh for doing such a great job helping me polish this book.

And I can't forget to mention Hiraida Diaz for her continuous support and the brilliant ideas that she has contributed to The Hero Within series.

This has been a very long ride for my family, but the reward is worth the wait. Thanks to my daughters, Yeiris & Tiffany, and my sons Bennett, Ethan and Nathan for staying by my side through this journey. You know I love you.

Table of Contents

"Yes, this is the path that has been given to us."
Judge paused and then said, quizzically "Did I ever mention that I know the book?"

"Could you be a little bit more precise, Judge?" Inquired Discerner.

"Well, you're going to laugh at this but, I *owned* the book for a long time, and I studied it too. But somehow after our last meeting the book went missing and I cannot imagine how it disappeared or why." Remarked Judge gravely.

"Did it ever occur to you to share that information with your partner, Judge?" Said Discerner, bitterly.

"Well, since I lost it, I thought there was no need to mention it."

"You are really one of a kind, Judge." mumbled Discerner.

"If there's one thing I *am* sure about it's that this old book is not in the prison facility."

"Very funny Judge. Stop with your jokes and let us get serious about this." Replied Discerner.

"Ok, you got me there, pal. I guess I could stand to shore up and stop kidding around so much, eh?"

The look that shot from Discerner's face was one of agreement, but it was tempered with affection and trust. Discerner slapped Judge on the back warmly. "Let's go, friend."

They searched all over the quarter of the city they had decided to start with, and there was no sign of the ancient tome. In fact, there were no books in the entire city as far as they could conclude from this and previous searches.

"I'm exhausted. How are we supposed to find anything in this ghost town?" Asked Judge.

"You mean, *ex*-ghost town. After we took it back from evil commanders and changed the name, people started moving in and improving everything." Mentioned Discerner.

"Yeah, everything except the locate-ability of literature..." Mumbled Judge.

Discerner looked up from the heap of ruble he was digging through with exhaustion on her face, clearly unamused with the joke.

Seeing this, Judge threw up his hands and tried to lighten the mood, "You are always right, and I am left." Laughing.

Discerner smiled and her countenance mellowed. They continued working through the moldering cityscape.

"You know, now that I think about it, I heard the women at the church talking about something called a "*mastaba*", and I felt embarrassed because I had no idea what that was. I had to Google it." Said Discerner, sheepishly.

"Well," Judge heaved as he threw another few scraps of refuse over his shoulder, "what is it? I've never heard that word in my life." Asked Judge in suspense as he placed his hands above his head to catch his breath.

"Welcome to the club. It means there is an ancient Egyptian tomb somewhere in the city. The bad news is that it must be buried somewhere." Replied Discerner.

"An ancient Egyptian tomb, buried somewhere... meaning underground?" Wondered Judge aloud.

Discerner looked over with a cocked eyebrow and a look on her face that seemed to say, "Well that's what *buried* means."

Judge exclaimed, "No way, you've gotta be kidding me! Now, I get to deal with mummies? Great! I'm about to be mummified."

"You know, Judge, and I am serious when I tell you this," said Discerner between breathes, "You are a total clown."

"Now that you mention it, there was something that looked like an ancient tomb in the book; I noticed it shortly after obtaining it, but I don't think the book could be in there. I know it seemingly disappeared, but it can't fly and bury itself in a masta…" he struggled, "mastaba? Yeah! That's what I was saying. But since it's the last place left to look I will give you the benefit of the doubt. Though, again, I don't think it will be there."

"Wait a minute, wait a minute. After all this time, and after all we've seen together, you think *that's* an improbable outcome? C'mon!" Discerner scoffed incredulously.

"What?" Judge said as he stopped to sip on his canteen. "I'm just saying that I don't think the book dematerialized and popped its way into an ancient Egyptian crypt for the sake of a gag."

"*You* just don't want to go underground."

Judge had nothing to say to that. Discerner was right, after all. He hated caves and crags and dark places; Cosets and even some buildings gave him the creeps, even to the point of anxiety. There was no explaining it as far as he was concerned, and it had plagued him all his life.

"Look, it's our best lead so far and it'll get us out of this dust and dirt for a while. What do you say?" Said Discerner earnestly.

Judge pondered for a moment, took another sip of water from his nearly empty canteen and looked out at the setting sun. He screwed the lid back on to the canteen and looked back to his partner.

"All right."

"Yeah! That's the spirit!" Yelled Discerner.

"Don't make me regret this, please." Judge sighed.

"Don't you worry, buddy, this'll be easier than a trip to the library." Discerner smiled slyly before chuckling maniacally.

The two headed off back to the interior of the city to get cleaned up before going to the archives; if they were going to pretend at archeology, they were at least going to get acquainted with a few books while they were at it.

The next day, the two trotted down to the archives. These halls were restored after they took back the city, and now they were one of the best resources around for research and record keeping. Seemed like a good place to start if they were going to try and find an ancient tomb. After they spent some hours poring over the oldest records they could find, Judge got a hold of some old blueprints of the city, and maps of the outer countryside too.

"That's it! That's gotta be it, right there in the forest." Judge exclaimed as he pointed enthusiastically at the map.

"Yep, I'll say you're right. But look here." Discerner gestured to a reference to a strange rectangular structure that looked to be significant to their search.

Judge gulped and seemed to hesitate.

"What?" Said Discerner "You thought all this was just going to be reading and hunting up blueprints? C'mon, man, I don't have time to keep babying you like this. God is on our side. What're you afraid of, huh?"

"Look I don't know, OK?" Judge snapped. "I just hate the idea of being stuck underground, that's all."

Discerner put his hand on Judge's shoulder. "Hey, I'm sorry, I didn't mean to belittle you. But we can't afford to turn away from this mission. We will make it through this, I promise."

Judge's face brightened. "You're right, God is with us, and we have never before failed. We *will* be just fine."

With this newfound courage and resolution, the team set off toward the west boundary of the city where the great forest loomed in a dusky haze. It seemed, inexplicably, as though it had remained untouched by the ravages of the conflicts that had raged on in the city during its emancipation from evil. In fact, it looked almost entirely untouched. The deep, impenetrable green of the trees was foreboding and ominous to the pair that now traversed its border, and even Discerner had a moment of hesitation as she looked into the mirk.

Noticing this hesitation manifesting itself in Discerner's stance, Judge quipped, "Yeah, right? Not so crazy now, am I?"

Recovering herself, Discerner snapped back. "Oh stop it, I'm not afraid. Just look though...look at this. It's incredibly cool."

"Cool, she says. Yeesh." Judge murmured. "Well after you then, Mrs. *Cool*."

The two penetrated the border of the forest and started down what looked like a relatively well-worn game trail. The distances on the map made it appear as though it would be reasonably easy to traverse on foot, besides, the terrain wouldn't have allowed for horses or other conveniences.

They walked for about an hour over the rocky ground, occasionally having to double back when confronted with an impassable cliff face or unexpected gully. But at long last they found what seemed to be the spot. However, it was a sort of complex of stones, not just one building or outcropping. It was overgrown but still quite distinguishable.

"We're gonna have to find the exact spot. It'll probably be some kind of centralized stone or earthwork; maybe a pronounced entrance or opening in the structure. Just keep your eye out for anything significant." Discerner proclaimed.

The pair split up and divided the complex into quadrants; Discerner took the east two quadrants, and Judge took 'the west two quadrants. It was high noon before either of them spotted anything of interest. One would occasionally shout to the other, which would be followed by a disappointed "Never mind!" They met back up in the center of the complex after several hours of fruitless searching.

"What the heck, man. Not a thing!" Exclaimed Judge.

"I know, this doesn't make any sense. This is obviously the spot, but we've combed it up and down for hours, and nothing has come up. We must be missing something." Discerner sighed in confusion.

The two sat for a few minutes in despair, until suddenly, Judge's eyes lit up. "Hey! What's that?" He pointed energetically at a structure that seemed to be forming out of the rocks before their very eyes. They were exhausted, but the revelation they were witnessing revitalized them.

"It's the sun! We just had to wait long enough for the sun to align with the stones so that it revealed the entrance!" Exclaimed Discerner.

"This is going to be the dig of the century. I'm just gonna let you do all the work though." Said Judge in amazement.

"Very funny. Start digging." Retorted Discerner.

"Ok, it was worthy try." Replied Judge.

The work was intense, and the stones were massive. Much of it they couldn't move on their own, so they made a fulcrum and lever from some surrounding wood and materials to help move the heavy stuff. It was back breaking, but they knew in their hearts that they were making progress.

After hours of digging and excavating, the sun was beginning to set, but they had uncovered the rectangular shape indicated on the map.

"Naptime!" said Judge as he collapsed, exasperated onto the dusty stones.

"Nap!? What are you talking about?" Burst Discerner.

"My bad. I meant sledgehammer time." Judge giggled. "Here," he said, rising to his feet "I'll take care of it. It'll be my penance for subjecting you to all these terrible jokes." He smiled.

With a mighty swing of the hammer they had brought with them, Judge crushed the surface of the stone slab they'd uncovered, and there, revealed by the few rays of sunlight that beamed into the gloom, they saw a staircase, spiraling down into the darkness. Surprisingly, the stairs looked relatively clean for an ancient and abandoned mastaba. They turned on their flashlights and ventured carefully into the black crypt. At the bottom, in a small room dripping with condensation, they found something that looked like a sarcophagus.

"Don't tell me there is a mummy inside that thing." Said Discerner, shakily.

"I guess it's time to get *mummified*." Chortled Judge

"Stop the jokes, I beg you. I am kind of freaking out here, man. We are deep underground, inside an Egyptian mastaba, next to a sarcophagus which probably has a thousand-year-old corpse inside it, and you are still joking. I beg you." Said Discerner.

"Sure…" Judge relented. "Hey, wait a minute. Why am I the one who's calm here and you're the one shaking like a leaf?"

"I don't know and I don't care, just stop joking around. This is the real deal here."

• • •• • •• • •••

"Give me a hand." Beckoned Discerner.

Judge helped her crack the sarcophagus open, and, to their surprise, there was no mummy. There was *nothing*.

"Honestly, I'm relieved." Sighed Discerner. "I was literally about to shit myself." She thought that would have made Judge faint, but as Discerner turned around to see the result of her profanity, she saw that Judge wasn't even looking at her. He was looking straight past her, into the gloom of the crypt.

Discerner wheeled around to find out what he was staring at, and there was a golden glint in the faint light. It was the book. It wasn't the sort of book she expected, it was a golden book, like in the movies.

"Oh man! This has to be important. A golden book! I was not expecting something like this." Said *Judge*.

They immediately lifted the book from its resting place. When they managed to open the book, its cover being very heavy, what they found were pictures of people of all races, worshiping different deities of all types. In its pages they also found vague references to an enormous serpent-like creature. It looked like a snake *and* a wolf of some kind. In some depictions, it was shown devouring people in the book. Judge saw an inscription on one of the pages so tiny and faded that he could not understand what it said.

"Discerner, check this out." He said.

"It looks like some sort of ancient language. Let me get my magnifying glass." Said Judge, laughing.

"Knock it off with the jokes, man." said Discerner.

"No, I'm serious, my magnifying glass would help." Judge handed it over to his teammate. "All right, now, what does it say?"

Discerner was able to discern the meaning of the ancient text...

Only the one not afraid to die will find me.

Judge would have liked this book had it been directed at him. There was something he could not explain in the *vibe* of the book. He felt it was guiding him.

"Look at that," said Judge, "there is a big golden key in the spine of the book. And there's an inscription on it!"

"Inscription, eh? Decrypting time, Judge!" Exclaimed Discerner. "You never fail to make me laugh, even in scary situations like this one, you know that?" She remarked.

Stick to open

"You see, I'm not the only one with a sense of humor. Even the golden book is cracking jokes. Of course, you need to *stick it* in the hole to open the door." Judge said, exasperated. "But we need to locate the hole for this big golden key."

"Judge, let us pray about this, I have an awkward feeling and I don't want to continue without a prayer." Said Discerner.

"Alright then, a prayer it is."

The team was praying for wisdom and knowledge about this newly found book and golden key, and thirty minutes later, they were enabled to find the hole in the wall in the crypt for that big golden key. It wasn't difficult, the keyhole seemed to radiate a voice that beckoned them to it, and exerted a magnetic force on the key itself. The closer they got to the keyhole, the stronger the magnetic force became. They inserted the key and everything in the room seemed to blur and warp, and a wave of dizziness came over them. As Judge turned the key and heard the lock tumble in the door, they were immediately…

Chapter 2

An exceedingly small piece of land in the middle of nothingness, inhabited by the scum of society. Some call it the ghetto of Nede Land, a forgotten and forsaken region, good for nothing and desired by no one. When all the other Kingdoms want to get rid of their punks, thugs, ruffians, troublemakers, cowards and pushovers; this is where they dump them. Banished to *Till Rest Save* town. At first, it was a small town, but over the years it grew with the refuse and riffraff of all the other Kingdoms.

The only entrance to this Kingdom is on the border of Mock Fenk Fist Kingdom, and it is heavily guarded. The rest of the Kingdom is surrounded by a dense, impenetrable forest that no explorer has ever returned from.

When a new resident comes to Till Rest Save Kingdom, the custodians must obtain safe passage from Headmaster Narnish in order to cross the border and dump the new resident. While they are passing through Mock Fenk Fist Kingdom. Two special guards assigned by Headmaster Narnish accompany them until they reach their destination.

People at *TRS Kingdom* must face each day on their own, making a living with whatever they can find and grow for themselves.

Stories say that people used to fight all the time for territory, constantly trying to make the place where they were dumped to die or starve to death a better home.

This is the only Kingdom that is not watered by any of the great rivers, and it is the smallest of all Kingdoms, yet, despite even their lack of water, they manage to be a self-sustaining little Kingdom.

After many years of struggling and fighting among themselves, this little Kingdom managed to establish an internal organization of sorts as well, which halted further bloodshed. Newly exiled people gravitate toward outcasts from their own land and count on them for protection and resources.

There is a mixed population of different professionals as well, which has contributed to the sustainability of the Kingdom. Fertile soil has been cultivated and it is fit for a modest range of agriculture, which in turn supports livestock. But all of this is kept secret from outsiders.

Spies have been sent in over the years to find out how these wretches have survived, but they have not been able to do so. The leaders of each group have pledged to keep the secret, revealing it only to their most trusted people. It is said that the influence of one group, named Snaitsirch, grew exponentially during the ancient times when most of the population followed and accepted the creed of the Snaitsirch. They believe in only one God, the Creator of everything. Scilohtac Group managed to send word of their God to King Rosuled of Hont Well Kingdom. When he heard this outrageous word, he became tremendously angry. King Rosuled organized an expedition to wipe out every single person of the Snaitsirch Group and he successfully annihilated nighty five percent of the Snaitsirch population. Only those that were *secretly* part of the group managed to escape.

. . . .

After the massacre, the other Kingdoms continued populating Till Rest Save Kingdom with their refuse, thinking it was cleansed of troublemakers. Years after this incident however, the population began to grow once again, and the massacre faded into legend. Groups continued to grow, increasing the number of their adepts, including the remaining members of *Snaitsirch Group*.

Legends say that the Malsi Group claimed they were descendants of Babul–Ell Kingdom, which started a rivalry with Scilohtac Group, whose members come from Hont Well Kingdom. The confrontation got so violent at one point that none of the other groups wanted to intervene. On one fateful occasion, after the conflict had gone on for years, a particularly horrendous battle went on for days, leaving many dead, and the loss was unbelievable. On the eighth day of the brutal confrontation, a member of the Anatanas Group, whose members come from Newt Live Kingdom, and a member of Amrahd Group, whose votaries hail from Mock Fenk Fist Kingdom, were hurt in the fray.

These two parties then joined the battlefield, seeking revenge for their comrades. They did not know who to attack, the Malsi Group or the

Scilohtac Group, so they decided to join forces and wipe them both out. When they saw they could not accomplish this alone, they called the group from Loom Live Kingdom, the ones they call the Scitpeks to join the fight with them. Casualties numbered in the thousands, and it appeared that there was no way to end the conflict other than complete annihilation.

Then, when things seemed bleakest, a small group belonging to no Kingdom at all had an idea.

"Let us sit down with the leader of each group, and attempt to find a peaceful solution before we are all destroyed." All the groups agreed to the suggestion from what turned out to be the Snaitsirch Group. That day all the warring groups signed a treaty that established terms of lasting peace. The Dexim Group did not sign, as they did not like to ally themselves with others, but all others signed the treaty.

The continuous struggle for supremacy among the various Groups is the greatest threat to peace in the Kingdom. Moreover, if a person does not have a strong conviction about the rules and beliefs of his or her group, that person could be persuaded to betray that group. In this small

Kingdom, everyone must be absolutely certain of their loyalties, otherwise they might end up in the wrong party. There are common, neutral establishments and conventions in the Kingdom for trading and leisure activities, but loyalty is the currency of the realm.

• • • • • • • • • • • • • •

In this forgotten Kingdom, an incredible secret has sustained the population. They do not have a river to water the land, it is true, but the land itself is like a spring of water. Every night, a dense fog settles over the entire Kingdom, and in the morning the soil is wet and fertile, ready for any kind of planting that might suit the people. Green grass and sprawling plantations are part of the mystery in this small Kingdom. Some say that water comes out of the ground like a mountain spring; some people say that after the massacre of Snaitsirch Group the land became dry and barren, and still others think that it was the result of a curse from the gods for almost wiping out that group from the Kingdom.

At another point, not long ago, pestilence and starvation once again seized the land. Then the remnants of Snaitsirch Group, the ones that were hiding, came out publicly once again and decided to honor their ancestors. They prayed to their God and the soil became fertile again. From that day, Snaitsirch Group slowly began to regain the respect and acceptance of other Groups.

When someone from the other six groups receives the conviction to be part of the Snaitsirch Group, (or to convert, as they say) even though the other groups do not like it, they do not meddle in Snaitsirch's affairs. They are more afraid of the curse on the land than they are of losing followers. After all, it is just one follower, they think to themselves. Some say that Snaitsirch Group named the Kingdom Till Rest Save in ancient times because they wanted to save all the outcasts of the various realms, and the Kingdom was supposedly their stronghold from which they could orchestrate this goal.

• • • • • • • • • • • • • •

As a gesture of appreciation (or apology, depending on who you ask), King Rosuled declared that the leaders of Till Rest Save Kingdom could send their delegates and fighters to Hont Well Kingdom's yearly tournament. Most of the groups eagerly await this season now, to prove that their fighters are worthy. They train hard, hoping every year to win the tournament.

A month before the time of the tournament, every group selects their best fighter. All the fighters from all the groups must fight for a spot at the tournament. The last two remaining get to participate and represent Till Rest Save Kingdom in the tournament. They say that Snaitsirch Group never participates in any of the tournaments because they are people of peace and words, not of war and bloodshed.

....

There is an ancient prophecy in the Kingdom of Till Rest Save about a nameless warrior, a descendant of Till Rest Save's people, who will rise to fight all the other Kingdoms, bringing chaos and destruction upon Nede Land. After the destruction, this warrior will create a new Kingdom of peace and tranquility for all.

Others say that the prophecy speaks about *two* warriors that will come from a faraway land, challenging all the leaders in the Kingdom, destroying the decadence and creating one unified Kingdom of hope for all the people of Till Rest Save, and that they will obey these warriors.

The prophecies are an ancient motivator for the faithful among the peoples, and those who can discern the cycles and seasons of time are also enabled to judge when these prophecies will be fulfilled.

· · · · · · · · · · ·

No one wants to go *voluntarily* to Till Rest Save Kingdom, and certainly no one wants to *live* there unless they are taken by force. Further, Till Rest Save Kingdom does not have the right to call anyone in, like the other Kingdoms. They are lost. They have no standing among the other Kingdoms, no political weight or bureaucratic power or representation. The only honor they are afforded is participation in the tournament of power, and even this was a sort of placation affected by King Rosuled.

• • • • • • • ••

The Elite Commander spoke to the heart of all the warriors, conveying a powerful message.

"Go ye to the new Kingdoms, conquer, and wipe out evil. Take the message of the One True King with ye. Claim the spiritual realms of these Kingdoms for the Lord. You are bestowed with the Gifts of the Spirit, use them wisely."

The team members understood that they needed to find and learn about the ultimate weapons, those that will grant them their full power and access to unimaginable skills. They knew it was a treacherous path, but one on which they would learn as well. Their journey begins here…

"I was in the *Spirit* on the Lord's day… (Rev 1:10)."

Chapter 3

"My King, recently we been getting reports of too many scumbags frolicking about and we need to find a place to dump them to die. We cannot keep using the supplies of worthy citizens for the sake of just a few lost souls."

"Can't we just *execute* them?" Asked King Rosuled, rubbing his eyes in exasperation.

"Great King, it would be easier that way, but there are some among them that are loved by the people, and I fear that if we execute them, we may excite too much turmoil in the Kingdom; and considering this is the capital of Nede Land, that would not be a good thing to demonstrate in front of the other Kingdoms we are governing."

"Who are those you referred to as being *loved by my people*?" Inquired the King with a venomous tone.

"They were the ones speaking against you, my King; their stories found sympathetic ears in the Kingdom and they won the hearts of many. They are a passionate group that can convince anyone to be like them." Explained the King's Advisor.

"They call themselves *Snaitsirch,* and they are immensely proud of their name. They have pledged their lives to the "Living God" as they call Him."

"It sounds as if you admire them." Said the King with suspicion.

He leaned forward, "Are you one of these blasphemers?"

"N…no, my King and Highness, you are my only authority, and a god to me. I don't follow *their* God and I am not interested in following them either. I am only saying that we should keep the peace we have in the Kingdom." Replied the Advisor, bowing low to appease his King.

The King sat back slowly. "Alright then, in that case, we need to find a deserted place with no access points from anywhere in the Kingdom, and dump them there to die. Since you sound like you are advocating for them, you will be in charge of locating such a place, and that is my command. Now, let me be and get this done as soon as you find the place. Inform me when it is through. You are dismissed!" Said the King.

"Yes, your Highness." Replied the Advisor, and he departed.

"Why do I feel like I have been *punished* with this task? I had to open my big mouth as always. I will learn some day to keep my mouth shut and I am sure it will ease my problems when I do." Thought the Advisor on his way out of the palace, wringing his hands.

"This is not an easy task and I will have to travel to all Kingdoms to thoroughly search for a place like this; but what will happen to the King in my absence, who will take my place? Master, who could replace you? I don't think there is anyone like you to be the eyes and ears for the King." Said Tseirp, the disciple of the King's Advisor.

The Advisor replied, "Of course, you have been with me all this time and you are always there when I am advising the King, there is no one better than you to continue my legacy, my dear *Tseirp*. I will hand you over all the keys and the scrolls for your protection. Advise well the King in my absence, I am not sure how long I will be away in this quest. I must honor the wish of the King in this matter."

. . . .

Several months passed by and the Advisor to the King was still searching for the perfect place, visiting all the Kingdoms in the entire Kingdom of Nede Land. One day he was visiting Narnish at Mock Fenk Fist Kingdom, and they took a walk through a nearby field. Their conversation was so interesting that they lost track of the time. They crossed the river watering Mock Fenk Fist and were almost at the border of the Kingdom, when the Advisor saw what appeared to be a hidden spot in the trees, and asked.

"What is behind these big trees that I cannot see beyond?"

"This is the place where we raised the pigs." Narnish pointed out. "We have a portion of the land dedicated to female pigs and when they are pregnant, we move them there and leave them to have the piglets. Of course, once a day, we get them out to bring them to the river and drink, because there is no water over there and the soil is dry."

"Can you take me there to see?" The Advisor asked.

"Yes, of course, we are almost there. We have been walking for a long time and I lost track, I barely come here. There is a small path for the swineherd to pass with the pigs." They continued on for a little way and as they approached the path they were able to reach the gate to the small portion of the land, far away on the border of the Kingdom. They kept it that far away because of the smell of the herds.

"This is a very big portion of land, and there is only one entrance and exit. It looks more like a prison, in fact." Thought the King's Advisor to himself. "I believe I have found the perfect place for my King." That is when the King's Advisor shared his mission and quest in the name the King of Hont Well, with Narnish. At the beginning, Narnish was hesitant to have these people close to his land, but the persuasion became too great to resist when the Advisor offered thirty coins of silver for the lot.

Not only that, they would oversee the project and get favors from the King. Whoever the King was going to appoint to be in charge of this new prison or *life graveyard*, would be well taken care of indeed. At last the task given by the King was accomplished, now it was time to return to Hont Well and report to the King of the successful mission.

"My King, I have finally found the place you commanded me to find." The Advisor exclaimed with pride.

"What are you referring to? It has been almost a year since I sent you on a mission and I don't really remember what I sent you for. You know, I really missed your advice the first few months, but I must compliment you on the great job you did with Tseirp, he has proven to be worthy of your trust. But come, fill me in on this mission." Added the King. The Advisor gave all the details on the journey and what he had been doing for the past nine to eleven months. Finally, he showed the King a small sketch of the location for the new lot where they were going to dump the pestilential people.

"You have done an excellent job and I stand by your decision! We will buy the lot and use it for that purpose. Since you have done such a great job and there is no one better than you for this task, I will assign you as the guardian and builder of this place. I will send word to Narnish and a certificate of your ascension. You are to be part of Mock Fenk Fist Kingdom as my attaché, and you will remain there until you've completed the task. I have complete trust in your judgment, Kouken." Said the King, laughing heartily.

"He used my real name." Thought the Advisor, beaming with pride.

"You will have three months to vacate all the pigs and create a few huts for the thugs you will throw in there. Understood?"

"As you command, my King." Replied Kouken in a surprised and sad tone of voice. "What have I done to deserve this? I have been demoted from the great capital to deal with pigs."

Three months later, Kouken was back at the capital with great news for the King. He was so happy because his task was finally over, and he was going to return to his old post as Advisor to the King.

"My King, the mission is accomplished! We have created the perfect spot for the scraps of the Kingdom. You may send the prisoners there whenever you wish, your Sanctity." Said Kouken.

"Congratulations on the excellent job you have done. I will surely reward you for this." Said the King. "As a token of my appreciation, you will be permanently appointed as the guardian and overseer of this project. In fact, I will give orders to have all prisoners ready so you can escort them tomorrow. You know the way, and you are responsible for this great work. I am proud of you." Added the King and slapping the Advisor on the back.

"Why don't I feel honored with this task? Is this my ultimate punishment?" Wondered Kouken. That day, he made a promise to himself. "I shall never return to my former position or to this Kingdom if the King does not beg me to come back. He will need me more than he can imagine, I will make sure of it." Thought Kouken to himself.

Chapter 4

There were approximately fifty prisoners to take to the lot which had been assigned for them to die in. There were men and women, and almost forty percent of them were in jail because of their heresy toward the Kingdom or because they rebelled against the practices of Scilohtac. Their crime was to claim that they could not bow down their heads to any image or man, that they could only kneel down and worship their *True* and newly found *God.*

They were looking for wisdom and reading the ancient book; the one that could only be read and interpreted by the Advisors of the King in their liturgy, and on top of all this they were inciting the people to riot and convincing them to accept their way. That was a crime punishable by life in prison and, sometimes, death.

"You wanted to incite my people, bring distrust and division in my Kingdom. You were reading the Holy Book without my permission and interpreting it for yourselves. I have found the perfect place for you to spend the rest of your lives, and as a part of your sentence, you may have your Holy Book so you may die with it." Said the King to the group of prisoners that were sent to die.

When Kouken arrived with the news about his permanent position imposed by the King, Narnish was pleased with him, staying by his side.

"Welcome, my friend, I am glad you will be a resident of this town. We might even call it a Kingdom soon. With your help," he said, reaching to embrace his friend, "I am sure we will achieve it." Said Narnish in happiness.

"And what will we call this place for the scraps of society?" Inquired Kouken.

"Let us follow the orders of the King and throw them there. As a sign of pity, I have left them a few pigs so they can survive a little longer and have them decide what they will call this forgotten and lost prison that will be their permanent home."

Since the majority of the people, or prisoners, belonged to this new group called *Snaitsirch*, they decided that day to call it "Till Rest Save." They set a goal in their minds and hearts to win the few remaining souls for the Lord and save their souls from damnation. The goal was to share with them the Holy Book and the only Savior un*til* the **Rest** of them would be **save**d.

Kouken and Narnish threw them in the small town of Till Rest Save and forgot about them, and it was time for Narnish to celebrate his new partner and forget about the scum of society, but not before saying some weird words that only he could understand. Afterward, they sealed the entrance of that lot, thus ensuring there was no access at all. Whoever wanted to gain entry would need permission from Narnish, and, moreover, the enchantment would only work by reciting it from the Mock Fenk Fist Kingdom side.

• • • • • • • • •

The leaders of Till Rest Save, were the focused type, and they were filled with faith in their God. They started preaching and sharing the Holy Book with the other people in the town and they were able to win them all for the Lord. That is about the time when the land started to act differently. A wet fog started to appear at nighttime, covering the land and wetting the ground, turning the desert like landscape into a mossy wetland. Grass started to grow, and the soil started to produce all types of fruits, but no one knew about any of this from the outside world.

Time passed, and King Rosuled had been the only one sending scraps to this place, when, one day, as had happened many times before, some citizens were pointed out as needing to be removed from Mock Fenk Fist Kingdom, and they were dumped in the same lot.

Word came to the other Kingdoms about this new prison and they started requesting meetings with King Rosuled, that he might grant them the opportunity to send their scraps of people to the same place. They even offered to pay for the trash people in their Kingdom to be thrown into this place to meet their final days, and King Rosuled agreed to fulfill the requests of all the other Kingdoms and began to collect one silver coin for every single person or prisoner to be thrown into this portion of Nede Land. All Kingdoms but one was paying tributes to get their disposal taken care of, the only Kingdom that was not paying for this service was Mock Fenk Fist Kingdom, since they were the hand of the butcher, the King.

They were disposing of men, women, children and entire families. These actions made all the Kingdoms pledge their loyalty, as a result of fear, once again to King Rosuled for finding such a great solution to this pervasive problem, and this helped him solidify his place in Nede Land. Finally, they had a common denominator other than power and it was the scraps of each Kingdom.

· · · · · · · ··

Days, weeks, months, and years passed by and the scrap-lot or, Till Rest Save, grew exponentially. What the other Kingdoms never thought about was the survival of the individuals they were condemning to this place. The more they dumped the more the population grew. People from all five Kingdoms of every belief and creed were being dumped there. There were those who were educated and uneducated; there were thieves, robbers, assassins, embezzlers, murderers, and politicians; there were innocent people, and there were guilty people, crazy and sane people; religious types, fascists, and freedom lovers, and any and all other "defective" people from society could be found in Till Rest Save.

The religious types were the most common in Till Rest Save, and consequently each one of the Kingdoms agreed to have a code name for their scraps, deciding to name them after their beliefs. The scrap of people coming from Hont Well were called the Scilohtac. They decided to call them this because people would never recognize the hidden meaning in the name, nor think of something like this for the kind of activity these people engaged in.

The scraps from Babul Ell were called *Malsi*. They named them so because they were radical and ready to sacrifice themselves to their gods; they would not hesitate to be martyrs.

The scraps from Mock Fenk Fist were called Amrahd, because they believed in the laws of the universe and the power of the mind.

The scraps from Noom Live were called *Scitpeks* because they do not believe in anything but their science and the power of proven facts.

The scraps coming from Newt Live were called Anatanas because they believe in the eternal order and they abide by their traditions in all their ways.

Among all of them, there were two main groups, called the "*Dexim*," which were formed by the outcasts of any of the groups; those that did not fit in with any of the other beliefs, or those who could be compelled to believe in anything.

The other group, which was the founding group of Till Rest Save, was called *Snaitsirch*, of whom you have already heard. They do not believe in any other gods other than the one True God, the Lord Almighty. That is their creed and their crime.

Chapter 5

Among the fifty original prisoners that were transported by Kouken to Till Rest Save, there was one group, a family who was the most devoted and faithful, head of the Snaitsirch group, that were taken because they were preaching about their new God and giving people free salvation. That action infuriated the King so much that he almost had them beheaded, but the people were so keen on and fond of this family, that the King could not find the perfect excuse to execute them. Sending them to Till Rest Save in the first wave was the best solution for King Rosuled. It was politically sterile and *neat*."

The head of that family was a very charismatic and gracious man named Yer Siul, who was imprisoned with his devoted and faithful wife, Anirefes. They were a young-adult couple, and very much in love.

Yer Siul was the type of person who is likable at first sight, he was charismatic and friendly, and possessed an incredible patience. He loved to play all kinds of games with children and with adults to make friends and acquaintances, as that was his way of reaching out to others and bringing them to their inner circle; this served the one True God. Yer Siul was incredibly wise and very good with numbers, but this prevented him from learning the art of writing and reading. He was persuasive nonetheless, and his knowledge could impact and captivate others within moments of meeting him.

On the other hand, Anirefes, his wife, was the perfect loving wife and mother. In fact, she was considered the mother of them all. Her charm and charisma drew people together and unified them under this perfect canopy of love. They formed the perfect combination of people for convincing and bringing others to their circle.

After they entered the scrap-lot and named it Till Rest Save, they were considered the heads of the town, which contained fifty people at the time. They started propagating the divine ideas and populating the town with converts. Yer Siul and Anirefes sired ten children, five sons and five daughters. Among them there was one called Naliolf, a strong and smart child. At a young age, he started working the fields and helping his parents raise the other nine children.

When Naliolf was of age he was betrothed and married to Atram, and at this time Yer Siul and Aniferes were graciously leading the new town, which created a safe enough environment that their sons and daughters could start procreating as well, which helped populate the town with even more of the faithful. During this time, Naliolf and Atram begat another son and they named him Rotceh.

Naliof was the type of person that, when projecting his voice, anyone in the entirety of Till Rest Save could hear him; he was able to reach anyone, anywhere with his voice. Some say that his voice was so strong that people from other Kingdoms used to hear his voice in the form of thunder.

Years passed by and new generations grew in Till Rest Save, and these began to forget the roots of the land and why they were placed there. They started inciting riots anytime a newcomer was brought to the town, and through this unrest they managed to spark the attention of the nearest Kingdom, the people of which granted them audience. This Kingdom was that of Mock Fenk Fist.

Narnish, as the head of Mock Fenk Fist, and Kouken, as the founder of Till Rest Save, (of course people did not know that he was the founder and builder of the town) were shocked with the news and the demands of this new town.

During all this, Yer Siul and Anirefes organized a festival in commemoration of the arrival of the first King into their town, someone who they thought would hear their demands and give them answers.

When Narnish and Kouken entered the barren and dried-up land they had allocated for the scraps of the Kingdoms, they were speechless; to see the lush vegetation, the green fields and swineherds was shocking. For years they thought that people were dying with no outside contact, but they were mistaken.

They could not believe their eyes as they listened to the demands of this new town, but at the same time their minds were drawn to the fields and the people. How could they have become numerous, building an entirely new town? When the vegetation did grow in this barren and dry land, it never grew like this. "Why now?" Thought Narnish to himself.

All they could say in response to their demands of being treated like human beings and to be given limited independence was "*We will discuss this further with the other Kingdoms and we will come back in three months' time.*"

The town that started with fifty citizens was now, forty years later, populated by approximately three thousand citizens, and they wanted recognition. After all, they could have a small army in the town and the other Kingdoms would not know it.

The leaders of Till Rest Save, Yer Siul and Anirefes, were pleased with the results of their first meeting with the King of the nearest Kingdom.

After nearly fifty years Kouken was now about to head back to Hont Well with a disturbing message for King Rosuled. At first, Kouken was angry and infuriated with himself for allowing such a thing to happen. "How could I have missed this, bringing this shame to my name? This time, it was not my mouth but my negligence." He thought.

"I fear the worst." In that moment, he organized all his thoughts and said, "But this is not all bad, this is actually good. The King forsook me, and this is a consequence of *his* actions, not mine. I will head to the Kingdom and deliver the news myself. I want to see the face of the King when he learns that a new town and possibly a new Kingdom will emerge as a result of his actions."

"Your highness, there is someone here to see you, he is requesting a proper audience with you." A messenger said to the King.

"And who is this person that wants to meet with me?" Asked the King.

"It is Bouken." Said the messenger.

"Bouken," thought the King. "why him?"

In a loud and suspicious voice the King said, "Bring him in, I want to know what business he has with me." When the King saw the man walk in, he rejoiced and shouted, "You foolish servant, you have mistaken the good name of my old friend and Advisor Kouken! Come and sit, Kouken. I am sorry they did not understand your name, so I did not know it was you." The King apologized. "You should be hungry and tired, let us go to where you can eat in the palace and we can speak as friends for old time's sake."

"Yes, your highness." Replied Kouken, bowing low. King Rosuled found it strange that Kouken called him "highness" instead of Sanctity, but he did not mind. "It *has* been many years." Thought the King.

After eating and drinking some ale, there was finally time for the bad news to be leveled at the King. When Kouken gave him the news, he thought that the King was going to be furious with him and have him decapitated; instead, the King laughed and said "Good job! Very well done indeed, my friend. I sent you out on a mission and you bring me a new Kingdom. I wish all my servants were more like you."

Kouken could not understand the reaction and was a little skeptical when the King added,

"I will go there personally and declare their limited independence; of course, they will all have to be subject to me and pay taxes as all the other Kingdoms do!" And an evil laugh came out of the King.

"Go, and give them the good news; I am partially granting their request, they will be acknowledged as something more or less like a small Kingdom. We will celebrate with a modest ceremony three months from now. I also want to see the vegetation and plantations you've described to me. Haha! Marvelous, Kouken!"

Kouken was not fully aware of the real intentions of King Rosuled, and he thought the best of him, even after hearing the crooked, evil laugh.

"You mention that they have two leaders, is that correct?" The King continued.

"Yes, they do." Replied Kouken.

"Perfect, I will procure appropriate gifts for them. You may depart and organize everything for my arrival. Make sure Narnish is present as well. Either way, he has to accept it, we bought the land, didn't we?" The King laughed again.

"Yes, we did, your Highness." Said Kouken nervously. The King noted something different this time when Kouken answered, but he did not know what it was.

Chapter 6

Yer Siul and Anirefes were conquerors of souls and giants of their faith. Having arrived at a young age in Till Rest Save and building a town, governing the population and increasing their numbers over the years had not been an easy task. What gave strength to this couple was their faith and their hard work with each one of the families. When they were exiled, the King placed in their hands the Holy Book thinking they were going to die with it. But instead, the Holy Book gave them strength and wisdom to govern, and most importantly, the power to win seventy five percent of the population at that time.

It was not an easy task changing the old views of the newcomers from their evil and idolatrous thoughts. They were coming from all the other four Kingdoms and they were damaged beyond repair, or so their butchers thought. But Yer Siul and Anirefes did not give up. They had to change the wrong beliefs of all the groups so people would accept and come to serve the only True God.

· · · · · · · · ·

Narnish was reluctant to accept the new changes, but he did not have much choice. It was either accept them or start a war with the main capital and King Rosuled himself. Even though it was not an easy decision, the outcome was obvious. Partial acceptance of their independence. Who would have thought that the land for swine herders could become a Kingdom? "If I'd thought this would happen, I would not have sold that land for thirty coins of silver." Thought Narnish.

• • • • • • • ••

Three months later, they were gathered at Till Rest Save in the presence of *two* Kings this time. King Rosuled and King Narnish, or *Headmaster,* as he preferred to be called.

They were welcomed and well attended with food, music and some honey ale, locally made.

"My Kings!" Shouted *Yer Siul*, standing. "Everything you see here is produced here, on our land. It has been cultivated, grown and harvested by all of us. We are not asking much today; we are only asking to be recognized as a small Kingdom in Nede Land."

With this, Anirefes also stood, and the entire town stood with her.

In a lyrical yet powerfully vibrant voice, she said, "We want to keep our name, and pay tributes to your Kingdom, King Rosuled." She intended to make it clear that their message was directed at one King only.

"Woman, sit down and let me do the talking." Mumbled Yer Siul, indignantly.

"What are you talking about?" She scorned, "You don't know how to speak, you will mess it up. Don't you shush *me.*" replied Aniferes to her husband, afterward continuing her speech.

"We will abide by your terms and conditions and we will be subject to your Kingdom. Please, just allow us the opportunity to show you our appreciation."

"You speak well, woman." Said King Rosuled, feeling flush with exaltation, and praised with all the words Aniferes was directing at him. "I came here today to give you your freedom and declare your town the Kingdom of Till Rest Save!" He shouted in a commanding tone with his hands thrust into the air. Everybody started applauding at these wise words from the King, and the atmosphere was more charged and optimistic than before.

"You have inspired me today to do more than that, however." The King continued.

At this moment, the King got down off his seat and called Yer Siul and Aniferes to approach him. "Come closer, and kneel before your King."

The couple said a silent prayer before moving to obey the King. "Lord, please forgive that we are kneeling before this man today, but it is just one knee and it is for the sake of the people."

The King drew his sword as they knelt in feigned loyalty and tapped each of them on the right shoulder. "I proclaim you King Yer Siul, and Queen Aniferes. Rise, rise and be baptized for your new Kingdom!" The crowd roared with excitement.

And so, they rose and received a baptismal sprinkling of water upon their heads, after which the King moved to close the ceremony; after all, no matter how enlarged his ego had become during the speeches of the two new "monarchs" he still despised them as vehemently as any of what he called his inferiors, and wanted to end this spectacle.

"As a token of my appreciation," said King Rosuled, "I am giving you this sword, the sword of a King." And he handed it over to the newly made King, Yer Siul. "And since you have shown yourself to be a fearless warrior, I am giving *you,* Queen Aniferes, this sword." The King thought that no one would ever think to come here, to this God forsaken Kingdom, to look for these two Holy Relics. But he did not utter a word and did not tell anyone about the truth behind these two swords, he only disclosed them to be the swords of a King and a Queen, nothing more. His true motive was well hidden in plain sight.

The commotion was so great that everybody forgot the other terms and immediately started celebrating in a furor of jubilance. That was it, ostensibly, the new King and Queen had been able to negotiate a deal that allowed them to start trading some of their products with Mock Fenk Fist Kingdom. They would receive compensation that was not exactly fair, but it was a start, and it was better than nothing at all, which is what they had been suffering with up until now. It was the first business transaction of the Kingdom and they were content.

The border of the Kingdom remained the same, however, and only the head of Mock Fenk Fist Kingdom was permitted to decide who would gain access and who would leave Till Rest Save. It was only partial independence they had been granted, after all, and it would be a terribly slow process toward full sovereignty, they knew.

• • • • • • • ••

Several years passed by, and Till Rest Save Kingdom had become prosperous in wealth within their limitations, and most of all, they were a Kingdom belonging to the Snaitsirch group. At this point ninety percent of the population was part of this group and that number increased every day.

King Yer Siul and Queen Anirefes were getting old now, and their oldest son, Naliolf was starting to inquire about Kingship and the business of running the Kingdom. He was showing interest in being the King, while his other four brothers and five sisters were not extremely interested in the crown. Other people were filling his head with thoughts and ambitions, not all of them noble. He was one of a *weak mind,* and he was easily carried away by people's thoughts.

Envious people wanted to gain access to the throne of Till Rest Save to conduct not-so-legal business, but King Yer Siul and Queen Anirefes were real, genuine Snaitsirch, through and through, and of strong faith, and they would never allow illegal practices to go on that went against the only True God. This, of course, over the years, had begun to irritate Naliolf, and he became more impatient with each passing day. Naliolf found some evil friends to fill his head with poison, which created jealousy toward his brothers and sisters to go with his mounting anger toward his mother and father. Strong envy and a desire for the throne are a nefarious and toxic combination in the hearts of those who are prone to evil.

Every day that passed, Naliolf's pride and spite grew in proportion to one another, and though it was not yet visible on his face that he held evil thoughts in his heart, he sheltered them all the same. This group of friends he had surrounded himself with had annexed his good and faithful friends and polluted his very surroundings with malice and disloyalty.

"The Kingdom is growing, Naliolf, and ninety percent of the population are followers of your God." These evil friends would say to him. "If King Rosuled finds out about it, he will think that you will turn against him, and try to convince people from other Kingdoms to follow this God." While this was true, the way they would phrase these things to him tended to leave out the will of God and His plans for Till Rest Save, thus making it seem as though King Rosuled was to be feared.

"Some of you have gained yearly access to another Kingdom, and have ventured abroad, this might cause a big problem when you get to be the King." They would say. For some time this continued, and almost as if these friends could sense the emotions of the young prince, they would never let him be free of their presence for too long, lest he come to his senses or be heavily influenced by *virtuous* friends. Every time a few days would pass without them in his midst, when he was on official business or a royal outing with the family, the young man would indeed become softened in his rage and less irritable toward his family. But it would never last long, for as soon as he returned home, these evil friends would descend upon him like vultures and quickly rekindle these unsavory traits, reinforcing his bad habits and turning him further from the light.

One evening, they were all gathered to drink and speak seditiously of the King and Queen, and things seemed particularly negative.

"They just don't understand!" Naliolf shouted, rising from his seat and throwing a bottle of wine he had been nursing against a wall, shattering it into a million shards. "Things can't continue this way, always increasing the numbers of this silly group they hold so dear to their hearts. It's a stupid superstition and an outdated one at that!"

"Hahaha! You aren't kidding!" One friend confirmed.

"I mean, do they really think that King Rosuled won't find out, or that he won't be furious when he does? They're buffoons and they don't know they're leading the people into a death trap." Naliolf continued.

"Yeah, man," another doubter spoke up, "remember the legends? That group already got dang near wiped out once before. Why would it be good idea to keep it alive, much less cause it to thrive?"

"You're right!" Naliolf shouted in return, pointing his finger at the bot and hugging him hard around the neck. "If I were King, everything would be different, everything would be above water with the King Rosuled. He would reward me...reward all of us!" He shouted, and they all roared with glee.

That night they came up with a plan to safeguard the Kingdom, and win the throne for Naliolf. They were going to stir the crowd and disseminate false information so Naliolf would be named King of Till Rest Save. The plan was nefarious and cunning, and was sure to work, they thought.

This political poison spread quickly in the hearts of people, and within a few short months, riots broke out in the once peaceful streets. One of the evil friends of Naliolf sent word to Narnish to advise King Rosuled of the situation that was about to come unhinged and potentially spread into other Kingdoms. They knew *that* would get his attention.

"The King and Queen of Till Rest Save have been gaining support from other Kingdoms, and they have been winning more people to their cause." The message read. "Send help to quell this uprising."

When Narnish and Kouken heard the alarming news, they sent word to King Rosuled. They were not aware of the hidden agenda of Naliolf and his evil Advisors, however.

"I allowed them to have a Kingdom!" Rosuled shouted, slamming his fists down upon the table that bore the correspondence of Kouken. "I even granted them power and *this* is how they repay me! By trying to usurp my Kingdom and fill it up with the plague of their teachings and beliefs!" He slammed his fists upon the table once more and pummeled it into dust. "I will deal with them myself." Whispered an infuriated King Rosuled.

During this upheaval, King Yer Siul and Queen Anirefes were becoming alienated from the reality of their situation. They were not aware that something was cooking in their own backyard to destroy them. They knew there had been some riots and disturbances, but knew nothing of the magnitude of the protests. After all, this is a Kingdom of Snaitsirch and they all obeyed the Only and True God, or so they thought. They had become complacent in this security, but they were a Kingdom after all, a small one, and every Kingdom must always be ready for a possible invasion, or a war. They were not completely bereft of sense, though, and in response to this turmoil, they created a small group of guards to protect the Kingdom in case any problems from the outside world should arise. There was a special distress signal, one they never used practically, only while rehearsing in case they would have to use it one day.

Chapter 7

"I need you to be my knight of terror for an expedition I have conceived." Said King Rosuled. "I don't want anyone to know that it is *you,* or that two Kings went after a very tiny little scrap of land." Both Rosuled's hands rested upon the shoulders of this great man before him, his friend and ally.

"What are you talking about, King Rosuled?" Asked King Babul Ell.

Rosuled squeezed the armor plating on Babul Ell's shoulders. "It is time to wipe out that noisy and annoying group of blasphemers they call the Snaitsirch…once and for all." He spat with disdain. "And *you,* my most excellent friend, will be my dark horse, my angel of death among them."

"I will gladly accompany you if that is what you need of me." Replied King Babul Ell.

"I knew I could count on you. We will meet three weeks from now on the out skirts of Till Rest Save Kingdom. I have given specific instructions to King Narnish for this invasion, and this is the only way into that Kingdom."

· · · · · · · · · ·

King Yer Siul and Queen Anirefes were not the fighting type, they were people of words and words of power, not the words of the commoner. More like words of an inspired King. They could inspire people every single time they were ready to instruct and give sermons to the people.

They implemented discussion sessions of teaching every month during which they could discuss any possible issue in the Kingdom. At the same time, they utilized these occasions to share their faith with the community and win those that were hesitant to come to the faith of the Savior.

As for the Holy Relics, several years after they received the swords from King Rosuled, they decided to lock them in a secure place for when the time came to pass them on to their children, and no one knew the location but themselves.

· · · · · · · · ··

Word came to King Yer Siul and Queen Anirefes that there was a coup D'état being concocted behind their backs and that an attack was imminent. There was no time for discussion or diplomacy, they decided, things were too far gone. They were told of the plans and they understood that King Rosuled would not come seeking peace or a truce, for they knew him well. If there was one thing he hated, it was those who opposed his religion and beliefs, he could not stand the idea of losing adepts of his faith to anyone. Unfortunately, it was too late, by the time they learned about this situation, the enemy was already at their door. In the day, which was already thick with sounds of destruction and violence in the streets, an eerie siren that no one had ever heard before began to wail.

"Why is the distress signal sounding? Are they rehearsing in the middle of the day?" Wondered the citizens of Till Rest Save, in such disbelief they were.

The group of conspirators gathered along with Naliolf and waited for the invaders to come. In their minds, they were only going to dethrone the current King and Queen and crown the new King as the successor. Additionally, Naliolf planned on pledging the Kingdom to Rosuled and preaching his creed and belief instead.

"Welcome," said the group of conspirators as the battle formation arrived, "we are not with them." The three Kings, Narnish, Babul Ell and Rosuled were at the gate of Till Rest Save. No one but the King knew about the real identity of the unspeakable warrior by their sides, not even Kouken.

They did not pay much attention to the message of the conspirators, and entered the Kingdom with full force, annihilating everything in their path.

When they found the King and the Queen, they killed them without hesitation and without remorse. Naliolf was expecting to be spared, but he did not know that the conspirators had wanted the throne for themselves all along.

"He is one of them, he is the elder son!" They shouted, betraying him. The Kings killed him instantly, or so they thought, and they dragged all the other members of the royal family out into the cold streets and massacred them along with ninety percent of the population; every single one that claimed to be Snaitsirch was butchered by this expedition, or *crusade*.

The little son of Naliolf, who was almost six years old, struggled heroically against the usurpers, hitting and striking out against the King's guard. At that moment, the unspeakable warrior saw the courage of this young boy and he fell in love immediately. That boy was the one they called

Rotceh, and he was spared and taken by the very same man that butchered and massacred his family, the unspeakable warrior. On that day, the royal family along with almost the entire population, perished. The few that remained pledged their allegiance to King Rosuled and his creed to save their lives. The Snaitsirch group was completely wiped out from the Kingdom of Till Rest Save. King Rosuled searched all over and had everyone else search for the swords of the King and Queen, too, with the promise that he would crown a new King and keep order. Since they were not able to locate the swords the King got so angry that he left the Kingdom to its own destiny.

"At least no one knows where the swords are; perhaps they were buried in the rubble of that stinking place, and that is well." Thought King Rosuled.

The Kingdom was left in chaos and disaster, the few remaining tried to keep order, but they were all envious and vicious men, they were not of the faith and creed of the Snaitsirch group. They did not believe in the True God nor had they the wisdom of the former King and Queen and that was the end of the dynasty of the royal family, at least that is what everybody thought.

Chapter 8

The other Kingdoms continued dumping their living cadavers in that Kingdom, or whatever was left of it. Years passed by, and still no order emerged nor did a clear leader arise to take the throne in the Kingdom. They were all fighting amongst each other and vying to keep control of their small tracts of land. During this time of chaos and squalor is when each one of the fanatic groups grew and gained influence. Each one of them assigned their own leader, and he in turn sought for an opportunity to defeat the rivals.

Not only did the people suffer, but the land did as well, which exacerbated the unrest and hostility; the soil became barren and dry as it had been at the beginning of time in Till Rest Save. People were starving and dying, and it got so bad that the strong began to eat the weak in ferocious and hideous acts of cannibalism. One day, there emerged two women, and each had a child. The one said to the other, "Let us eat your child today and then we will eat mine tomorrow." The one agreed and when the time came to eat the other child, the other refused. These words and actions left a deep scar in the hearts and minds of all the residents who refused to commit such acts of barbarism.

They had lost hope completely, and just as the light was about to be completely extinguished, a few good men who still stood in the Kingdom, those who were also secretly a part of the Snaitsirch group, decided to speak up.

These men had found the secret and forbidden Holy Book that was kept intact after the annihilation, and, learning from the Holy Book, they gained wisdom and knowledge. In fact, there was still one of them alive from the previous inquisition, and now he spoke.

"We have wronged the land and we have wronged God, the only True God. We allowed outsiders to invade our Kingdom and butcher our King and Queen." They thought. They believed everyone had been out, everyone belonging to the Snaitsirch group. "But today, we stand firm, and we are proud to speak out against the evil deeds and thoughts of your hearts."

Another of them stood to speak.

"Even the land has paid the price for the treachery we've committed against our former King and Queen. Our *God*, the *Almighty God* is angry with us, but if we repent and seek His forgiveness, He will restore the greatness of our land and it will produce fruit again. If you don't believe our words, you will believe our actions today."

Yet another stood to speak wisdom.

"We pray today to the *Only God* and *Lord* of our hearts with hearts of repentance and forgiveness. Father," he continued in a reverential voice, "forgive our past transgressions and turn your eyes upon us one more time! Bless this Kingdom as you blessed it before; we asked you today to show your power to this incredulous people. In Thy name we intercede for them. Amen."

The other groups did not see any sigh or even the smallest reaction, but they did not have any quarrel with these few men, so they did not believe their words.

When the night came, nothing happened. And on the second day, nothing happened, so one of them spoke again in public in a loud voice. "Lord, don't leave us alone in this moment of distress!"

The Snaitsirch group continued praying and pleading to God Almighty. On the third night, the fog came and covered the land with freshness, watering the soil and renewing some crops. In the morning, the grass was starting to grow, plants and vegetation were starting to sprout and the few people of the Snaitsirch group started screaming and waking everyone up with the noise and commotion.

"*Our Lord* and *God* has answered our prayer, He has heard us! Wake up, get up, come and see what our *Lord God Almighty* has done for us!" They shouted. "He has blessed the land where we are living, we will no longer suffer. Come and see."

That day, many believed and came to accept the creed and faith of the Snaitsirch group. They all started fearing the group because they prayed, and the land was healed. They immediately understood that their past transgressions were the reason the land had been cursed. They did not want to see that curse ever again in their land, so they started respecting and accepting those of the Snaitsirch group.

On that day, the people made a pact with the Snaitsirch group and their God to respect the creed and faith of the group and if anyone from any of the other groups were to be convinced or persuaded to be part of the Snaitsirch group, nobody would try to interfere with them. They were welcome in the Kingdom once again since there was just fifty men, women and children belonging to their group, but what everybody feared the most was the curse.

But there was still division and fighting among them, and thus there was no chance of having one concord for choosing a new King. They all wanted the position of the King of Till Rest Save, so, they remained a Kingdom without King.

King Rosuled sent word to the citizens of Till Rest Save that they were allowed to participate in the Soultai Tournament once a year, and that this was their only time to open the gate of Till Rest Save to the world. They felt honored and they felt that after many years, they were remembered by the King. Alas, they did not know that King Rosuled did this because of his shame, the shame that he bore for annihilating almost the entire population of a subject Kingdom.

Every member of every group was happy, and the Malsi, the Scilohtac, the Anatanas, the Amrahd, the Scitpeks and even the Dexim group started training their chosen warriors to qualify and participate at the Soultai Tournament. Every group, that is, with the exception of the Snaitsirch group; they were not going to enter the tournament. They became great fighters and masters of the arts of fighting with the single purpose of winning the Soultai Tournament, but Snaitsirch group was not into violence or fighting, they were people of peace and God.

• • • • • • • ••

Years later, the Kingdom was able to learn the truth behind their tragic story of butchering the royal family and wiping out all descendants and heirs to the throne from the face of Nede Land. The stories always mentioned that Naliolf was deceived by evil friends. One of Naliolf's best attributes was the care he had for his family, his wife, sons and daughters and especially for the small one. He used to play all day long and take him everywhere he went, the one they called Rotceh. It was a great shame that all the family members perished.

Chapter 9

Many years passed, and they all forgot about their past transgressions and the unforgettable actions against the Snaitsirch group. Their Kingdom grew once again and a new generation came to fruition, but a few families of the old generation were still present.

King Yer Siul and Queen Anirefes were long forgotten, only legends and part of history along with the massacre that the Kingdom suffered. There were only vague mentions of the long-lost swords of King Yer Siul and Queen Anirefes, the first and last ones to rule over Till Rest Save Kingdom. The legend says that only a direct descendant of King Yer Siul and Queen Anirefes could wield their swords. Such swords would give the users unique powers as long as the blood of the King and Queen was running through their veins, but that person does not exist, they thought, and they all lost their hope in having a King.

And yet, even when the land gained prosperity and a large population, the wickedness and evilness of the Kingdom increased every day.

• • • • • • • • ••

Only the Snaitsirch group was aware of the prophecy of Till Rest Save. The prophecy speaks about a nameless warrior, or warriors, direct descendants of Till Rest Save Kingdom, who will rise to fight all the other Kingdoms with the promise of justice, peace and everlasting prosperity.

The only entrance to the Kingdom was from Mock Fenk Fist, and it could only be accessed by Narnish himself, but the citizens of Till Rest Save Kingdom did not know of the mystery buried in the Kingdom. Till Rest Save Kingdom did not have any guard to keep their entrance to earth safe because no one would ever dare to cross that gate. There was no need for a lost and forgotten piece of land populated with a bunch of nobodies to have a guardian.

• • •• • •• • ••

The Holy Book was calling out for help, the Holy Book was calling and attracting someone from a faraway world who would be keen enough to hear its call and come to the rescue of Till Rest Save Kingdom.

Finally, the Holy Book was able to locate two worthy sets of keen ears to hear its call of distress and come to their rescue. These worthy ears were from another world, and were the least expected to come.

That is when Judge and Discerner started listening to the call through an incredible magnetic force pulling them into this new spiritual world.

And they were immediately pulled in and transported to the spiritual Kingdom of Till Rest Save.

• • • • • • • ••

"I think our call has arrived sooner rather than later." thought Discerner.

"We are already in the new Kingdom. We are now the Kingdom's people." Joked Judge. Discerner only looked at him out of the corner of her eye.

"Let us get moving and find out our task in this Kingdom. I was expecting something more glamorous for a Kingdom, even though the view is pleasant enough with the greenery and these old houses. I never thought a Kingdom would look more like a slum." She added.

"You surely are a woman; you have just arrived at this new Kingdom and instead of worrying about the danger that might await us, you are concerned about the look of the Kingdom. Women!" Said Judge, laughing at her.

While walking on the streets they bumped into a group of five dirty looking fellows. They looked more like gang members than average citizens.

"And who might you two be?" One particularly big man inquired.

"You look lost, you don't look like the normal type coming from the other Kingdoms. You are not one of the scraps they always throw in here." Another said.

"We are looking for the King of this Kingdom." Said Discerner, firmly. At the sound of these words, they all laughed uncontrollably.

"You have come a long way for nothing, lady." The big one replied to Discerner. "We've had one King and Queen and they did not meet a good end at all, as the story says. I am sorry to tell you that you came along way for nothing, but if you want to find your death wish, just continue walking the streets and you will meet your end soon enough."

They all continued to laugh heartily. One of the gang members stepped up and asked,

"But where did you come from and what are you doing here?"

Whispering among themselves, our duo overheard the conversation. "This must be a trap set up by the other groups; after all, we are the Scitpeks and we must not trust our eyes, let us examine the data and get to a conclusion before deciding what to do next."

But while they were discussing the matter among themselves, Judge and Discerner were long gone.

"What a strange people they were." Commented Discerner.

"Yup! They looked like circus clowns!" And they both laughed.

Now, the Scitpeks group was one of a kind. They were proud to call themselves descendants of Noom Live Kingdom and they've learned to trust no one and were always looking for a trap in everything. They did not believe in anything but the end results of large scientific studies and data, which they all lack at Till Rest Save, but they kept their customs, something not easy to change. In fact, they made it more like a religion to them and that was the appealing part of this group. Not believing in any deity or divine power if they could not prove its existence.

• • • • • • • ••

"Judge, did you noticed, this part looks different from the other? Even the color of the houses is different, and it looks like we are entering a new zone."

Part of the division of the groups was selecting a different style for each zone and mapping them with their favorite colors. The Scitpeks color was like a rainbow, or mixed colors creating the *notion* of a rainbow in their houses and across their zone.

This zone started at that house back there, and just changed shape and color. It is one color only. Sky-blue. Let us be careful." Commented Discerner.

"Yes, Sir Madam." Said Judge laughing.

"You are not going to start with your jokes, are you?"

"Not at all, Madam." Replied Judge teasing her.

"Stop it right there!" Yelled a man. "Who are you and what are you looking for in our zone? What group do you belong to?" The man continued with his line of questioning without giving them any time to answer at all.

"I beg your pardon, if you allow us to speak, we could answer your questions." Said Discerner, finally able to break through the monologue.

"Very well, woman." Replied the man, acting tough.

"We are looking for the leader of the town, the strongest fighter." When the man heard these words, he got scared and said, "Madam, Sir," tapping their shoulders easily, "there is no need to get violent here, we were just asking. This is the zone of the Dexim group. We are called this, because we don't really care much about the quarrels of other groups, and we are comprised of the ones who don't want to stay in any group. Having said that Madam, Sir, please continue your journey, we will not oppose to your quest." And the man bowed and gestured for them to move on.

Now, the Dexim group did not have a creed, per se, since they did not want to cage themselves with any of the groups, but there were people from every group and every Kingdom who respected one another.

"The zone you are about to enter, the Green cheese color zone, it belongs to the Amrhad group; they are the ones from Mock Fenk Fist Kingdom." The man concluded by saying.

Chapter 10

Discerner and Judge continued their journey, but they did not know what to expect.

"Well, I must say that I am impressed with this Kingdom, the people are very polite and they don't like violence; avoiding unnecessary fights is the best way." Said Discerner.

"I am very glad that we are not fighting our way in…because we were already in, get it?" Commented Judge, trying to crack another of his jokes.

"Very funny, Judge, veeery funny." Discerner replied sarcastically. "I wish you had never said those words. As soon as you mentioned not fighting, look what appeared."

When Judge raised up his eyes to see better, he perceived two warriors standing at the limit zone.

"Well, it *is* fighting time." Said Judge, smiling at Discerner.

The two warriors spoke in unison, and in a loud, slightly whimsical way, "We don't appreciate intruders and they are not welcome here. No one is allowed to pass! If you are not from this Kingdom, you cannot walk around like you were in your own house. You will need to fight us to get through."

Now, one individual stepped forward.

"I am *Uzad.*"

Then, the other stepped to the side of the first.

"And I am *Iyad.*" They then made a flashy display of their strength and their fighting style.

"We are the warriors of the Amrahd Group and we fight with the Mock Fenk Fist fighting style." They said in unison.

"What a weird name for a Kingdom." Said Judge.

"Are you trying to mock our pride and our Kingdom!?" Uzad shouted furiously.

"I don't get it, you said that you are from another Kingdom and yet you are here. Why are you not in your beloved Kingdom?"

"Judge, can you stop teasing them." Said Discerner.

"I'm just curious, aren't you?" Judge shrugged.

When the two opponents heard these words, they got even angrier and went head-to-head with Judge in a flash.

"Do you need any help?" Asked Discerner, watching Judge leap out of the way with ease.

"No, it's ok, I got this." He said cheekily as he winked at her.

They came with full strength and hit Judge so hard that he fell on the ground. They did not even allow him to stand before continuing to hit him with an incredible strength and immense violence.

"You *were* mocking us!" Yelled Iyad.

"Why don't you mock us now? I thought you were strong and look at you, already dead!" Chided Uzad. "But death is not enough for you!" They continued hitting him, and when they got tired of hitting him on the ground and making Judge bleed, they left him alone for a moment, thinking he was dead. They proceeded to Discerner.

"We will go easier on *you*, woman, since you did not disrespect us." They laughed in a sleazy tone and high-fived each other. "In fact, we are even willing to let you go unharmed if you apologize to us in the name of your partner."

"Fellows! I think you two are mistaken and have obviously wrongly assessed the situation. I am not the one in critical danger; it is *you*. You have made a big mistake by not making sure your opponent was dead. Instead, you chose to believe an illusion. Don't just stand here, go to your fight and leave me alone." Said Discerner waiving her hand in annoyance.

When they looked back, there was Judge standing with his body all beat up and his clothes torn, but on his right upper chest there was a visible number "5" and that number was glowing like fire.

"I don't know what kind of fighter you are and I don't understand why you are still standing," Said Uzad in astonishment, "but I will finish you off with one blow. Iyad, don't interfere."

"Right!"

Then, Judge said, "You made me angry and that is not good for you. Now you are trying to fight me one on one, you must be crazy. Or you must have a death wish. Either way, so be it."

When Uzad rushed to terminate Judge, he unleashed his powerful *Dao sword*, dripping with flames and energy, and *Uzad* was no more the moment the flames touched his body.

When Iyad saw that his partner was dead, this enraged him, and he lunged to finish Judge himself.

"What a foolish man. It seems like you people don't understand, or don't know your limits." Said Judge, showing his purple Spartan sandals flaming with incredible fire.

When Iyad went to touch Judge in an attempt to cut his head off with one blow, the flames emanating from Judge's body mingled with his Dao swords and curled around Iyad, constricting like a luminous snake, and he was no more.

The proud fighters of the Amrahd group were thus defeated without putting up much of a fight. They were no match for the anger of Judge. The other members watching the fight saw the incredible display of power and did not dare to cross the path of these two warriors.

Immediately, they sent word to the next group in line, the Anatanas, who come from Newt Live Kingdom.

When they heard word that two strong fighters were coming to their zone and that they had defeated Uza and Iyad, they were concerned. These two had the reputation of being the strongest in the Amrahd group and being defeated means that a big fight was on the way.

"But who are these two people and why are they fighting in our Kingdom?" Wondered Aved and Ived.

• • • • • • • ••

Aved and Ived were a couple of fighters that worked their way to the top of the Anatanas group. They literally fought their way up, giving up children and descendants to dedicate themselves to the goal of being leaders, trainers and masters of the Anatanas group.

"We will have the opportunity to test our strength on these two new fighters." Said Aved with a tone of joy.

"I have a bad feeling about this and these strangers; we must be careful." Said Ived in concern.

For the first time in her life, Ived thought about her life and the consequences of having no heir or descendant. "What will happen to the Anatanas group in Till Rest Save Kingdom and most of all, what will happen to us? There is no one we can leave to remember us, if something bad happens to us." Thought Ived.

"Darling, don't think about these things, we have given up everything to be where we are and we won't lose to these foreigners." Replied Aved, comforting her.

When Judge and Discerner arrived at the zone limit to enter the new area, they saw this lovely couple sitting down and waiting for them.

"Can I fight this time?" Asked Discerner. "You had your fun last time, I think it is time for mine."

"Well it was not that fun, since you got angry over a little scratch." She laughed.

"Agreed, darling."

"You will fight next battle and then it will be my turn again. It will always allow us to rest a little bit between battles that is if there are more battles to come. I hope they'll be more challenging next time, we are still fighting and searching blindly, and we don't know who or what we are looking for. But I am sure, the Lord will pave the way for us."

Chapter 11

"Welcome to Anatanas territory, you are about to enter a dangerous zone indeed! *We* are Aved and Ived, and we are in charge of the Anatanas group, and proudly hail from Newt Live Kingdom. There is no other option but to fight us if you want to continue on your path, wherever that might lead you." Shouted Aved with pride and conviction.

"Allow me to ask out of politeness, why did you come to our Kingdom and what are you looking for?" Asked Ived.

"We came to this Kingdom because we were called, and we are looking for the guardians of the Secret Relics." Replied Discerner, firmly.

"I think you have the wrong Kingdom, there are no guardians here, and no *secret relics*, whatever those are. You have come to the scrap bin or dumpster of Nede Land. The only good thing to have come out of this place is us, and we will defeat you; otherwise, the good people of Till Rest Save will succumb to darkness without us." Said Aved.

"Wow! You must be the saviors of this Kingdom, and powerful ones given the high opinion you have of yourselves, claiming to be the light of this place. We don't know much about your Kingdom, but one thing is for sure, there is no light coming from you, otherwise, you would have not ended up in our path, which leads to your annihilation." Replied Judge.

"Why do you always have to tease people into fighting?" Wondered Discerner. "Don't pay attention to my partner, you will be fighting me instead and I will be gentle with you two. I will just knock the so-called "light" off of you."

Hearing these words incensed Ived, who immediately prepared for the battle. She rushed Discerner with twin swords drawn and aimed to lob her head clean off. But this wild attack was meant with a crippling counterattack from the target.

"What are you doing, man? Don't just stand there, go help your wife! Otherwise there will be nothing left of her." Said Judge to Aved, with smarm.

At this warning from the enemy, Aved turned to confront Judge instead, but then he heard the cry of his woman, "She is too strong! Help me!"

"When he turned to help her, it was already too late…she was already gone. Discerner had used her Swiss Katzbalger sword and the righteous flames it produced to wipe out the enemy.

Aved was hurt, deeply, at seeing the dissolution of his wife, and he was rightfully angry. He immediately attacked Discerner, jumping with a crushing strength that he aimed at her head.

"You'll have to do better than that!" Judge shouted with hands cupped around his mouth. "You have to avenge your woman! Haha!" He continued, mocking him.

Aved increased his power to its limit and this time he was able to hurt Discerner when the blow landed squarely on her shoulder.

"Well, it looks like you had a hidden power." said Discerner. But what was standing now in front of Aved was a completely different knight than before; Discerner was now displaying a gleaming yellow silver belt radiating fire along with her Spartan sandals which sparked fire with every step she took.

"You are no match for me." Said Discerner, rising with her sword and combining the power coming from her new accessories to increase her power tenfold. With one blow and in a blinding light, Aved was no more.

Discerner started yelling with her arms outstretched, "Is there no one else? Is there no one else to fight me? Where is the light these two were talking about? I could only see darkness! *We* have light and we are bringing it to this Kingdom because the one who is with us is *The Light* of the world!"

"Calm down, said Judge, "it looks like there is not a worthy opponent in this Kingdom."

Upon hearing these words, everyone around who had been watching was confused and did not know what she was talking about. "They are bringing light and her partner is the light of this world?" They thought. "They are really two wackos, let us move away from here in fear of these two weirdoes." These were the thoughts of Anatanas group.

"Let us leave them to the Malsi group, they will surely handle them the way they deserve. They are as crazy as these two and if the Malsi don't take care of them, then the Scilohtac group will wipe them out for certain. We cannot even think about the Snaitsirch group, there is no hope in even thinking about them."

Chapter 12

King Babul Ell is known as the strongest

creature in all Nede Land and only the strong
stand by his side. Legend speaks about two great
warriors coming from Babul Ell Kingdom and
there are many speculations as to why.

As soon as Izar La and Hudba La arrived at Till
Rest Save, they started a fight with everyone
around them; they wanted to get this anger out
with someone, and they beat up every single
member of the Malsi group and placed
themselves at the head of the group afterward.

When Judge and Discerner saw the greenery in
this part of the Kingdom, they immediately
realized that they had crossed into another group's
territory. Standing in the middle of the street
there were these two fighters waiting for them.
And they said to each other,

"Izar La, I will take the one on the right and you
will take the one on the left."

"Agreed." Said Hudba La with a grin.

They did not want to spend any time placating or toying with these two intruders, they wanted to fight for real.

"It has been a long time since we've had a real fight, let us hope they are the real deal and can serve as a practice bag at least." Thought *Izar La* and *Hudba La* simultaneously.

They possessed an incredible strength that dwarfed the weaklings they had fought before; Judge and Discerner felt the impact of their initial attack and it was a heavy blow to their psyche. Finally, someone worthy to fight, said Judge.

"And here we go again." Thought Discerner. "You are going to start by teasing the rivals one more time; you never get tired of doing so." They hadn't finished talking when the second blow came down from the sky and this time, it was stronger. Judge and Discerner were bleeding from the ears and staggering back in shock for a moment.

"You have taken two blows from us and you are still standing. Impressive! I am *Izar La!*"

"And I am *Hudba La*. We will be the last thing you see today!" They said in unison. And then Judge said out loud,

"Welcome brother La, we have a music partner here!" And he began singing the musical tune "*dooo, reee, miiii, faaa, sooool, laaaa, tiiii!*"

He stopped and continued taunting them. "We get to play music now! C'mon, music boys!"

"Judge, how many times have I told you to stop teasing our opponents, they might end up singing a song instead." And they both laughed.

"You two think you are funny." Said *Izar La* as he lunged for the third time, hitting both Judge and Discerner at once. *Izar La* and *Hudba La* did not expect the results that followed. "Is it already over, we thought you were strong?" They saw blood drip on the ground as Judge and Discerner hit the dust.

"Why do they always make the same mistake? They see you down and they think they've won without even making sure the opponent is dead." Said Discerner quietly.

"Boys, don't get cocky on us, the battle has not even started!" Shouted Judge.

Standing up, Discerner now appeared as a totally different knight; she was displaying her yellow Spartan sandals with flames pouring out of them. Her yellow silver belt and a yellow diamond shield also materialized.

"I am Discerner, and I will be your opponent today." Addressing her words to *Izar La* as she leveled her sword at them.

Looking at Judge, they could now see purple Spartan sandals with flaming fire brimming over them, a purple silver belt and a purple diamond shield.

"I am Judge, and I will be your opponent today." Addressing his words to *Hudba La*.

"Now we are talking! I can feel your power and I am excited!" Said *Izar La*. "Woman, you are enormously powerful! I have been expecting someone strong enough to stand up to me."

"Well, no need to wait any longer, for I will not only stand to your challenge, I will beat you like you have never felt before." Added Discerner.

"Judge, are you mad?"

"No, I am not." He replied.

"Excellent, no need to get mad yet anyway."

They could not understand what they were talking about, but they did not want to figure it out, just yet.

Hudba La then said to Judge. "Shall we fight or watch the fight? You see, it has been many years since I've seen my older brother fight and I would love to watch his fight."

"Well friend, today is your day. I am not in a hurry and you are not going anywhere anyway, so, it would be interesting to see if your brother can keep up with Discerner." Added Judge.

"By the way, what was that about you being mad?"

"Don't worry about it, I expect you don't find out." He said with a grin.

Izar La and Discerner were two incredible fighters, and their speed and strength were almost equal. Suddenly, in the heat of combat, Discerner fell to the ground after deflecting one of Izar La's mighty attacks. She was hurt badly, bleeding and bruised.

"She is done!" Shouted Hudba La to Judge.

"Well, if she were a regular person, I would agree with you, but she is not at all the normal type; just wait and watch." Judge said as he leaned against a tree, folding his arms across his chest.

Discerner increased her level of strength and this time, as she lifted herself from the ground, not only did her yellow Spartan sandals, yellow silver belt, and yellow diamond shield burst with energy, she was now wearing a yellow bronze breastplate that was irradiating flames in every direction. She cracked her neck, her arms and her legs and said, "Now, let's play. Come at me with all you've got, Izar La."

And so he did; Izar La charged Discerner with frightening speed and let loose one of his most powerful attacks, but this time, Discerner was able to block it and with the strength of her guard alone she repelled Izar La and threw him a few feet away.

"She is stronger now; I'll have to use my full power to defeat her, the very same power I used to win the championship." Said Izar La in his mind.

He then increased his power to its limit, and descended on his enemy, thrashing Discerner around like a rag doll with his blows and left her for dead. He was about to celebrate the victory when Judge yelled, "Don't get too excited and don't celebrate, the battle is not yet over. At least not for her! I am not sure about you though."

When Izar La looked, Discerner was standing again and ready to fight.

Socked, Izar La stuttered and said, "But that was my most powerful attack, no one can withstand it twice! Who are you woman? What are you made of?" He inquired in complete shock.

"Don't worry, allow me to show you." Said Discerner. She suddenly, but with grace and elegance began to dance and chant a strange rhythm. "*I am the daughter of the Almighty and I come in His name, there is nothing stronger and greater than His power, my Lord and my God.*" Izar La was enchanted as he watched Discerner float around the battlefield singing these terrifying words in such beautiful harmony.

"What extraordinary power and grace." He whispered.

As he was transfixed, Discerner descended upon him with a furious attack that stunned his already entranced mind. He never stood a chance; Discerner annihilated him in an instant.

"My brother…" Muttered Hudba La, "I will surely avenge you."

"No so fast, my friend. I am the one to fight you, but if you want to avenge your brother, let me ask her consent first."

Hey you! That good looking and strong woman, filled with fighting adrenaline!" Said Judge, teasing her. Discerner was slowly drifting down from the air where she had been suspended after the attack she used to defeat her enemy.

"He wants to avenge his brother, he wants to fight you." Shouted Judge.

"I am pumping pure adrenaline now, so if he wants to fight, let him come." Remarked Discerner, casually.

"Are you sure you don't mind though?" Discerner asked Judge.

"No, it is ok. I am relaxing here, we have walked too much, and I am tired." Reassured Judge, waiving his hand.

"You lazy good for something, I will deal with you later!" Screamed Discerner to Judge. "Lazy man, on and off again." She said.

Turning to Hudba La, Judge shouted, "Pal, you got your wish, just be careful what you wish for, you might be stepping into fire, literately!"

"Are we going to fight or what?" Inquired Discerner, looking bored. This time, she had transformed slightly and was wearing a golden helmet in addition to the other accessories; she was now fully transformed into a powerful yellow knight.

"Be careful, my friend, her powers are at the limit, she cannot hold it back when she gets like this. I am warning you." Said Judge. But Hudba La only had the death of his brother in mind, thus he did not care about any warning or anything else for that matter; his goal was to defeat Discerner and avenge his brother. Even when he was younger, he got to be stronger than this brother.

"Come at me with all you've got," said Discerner, "or I fear the worst for you."

"Stop patronizing me! Stop your condescension! I will make you pay!"

He lunged for Discerner and leveled an attack at her that could've split a mountain, and it connected like a thunderbolt. She hit the dust, but rebounded and came right back up, hitting him harder than ever before.

"You are stronger than your brother, I will give you that, but I believe you are not serious about avenging him. Why don't you give me everything you have?" Asked Discerner.

"And you talk about me teasing my opponents, that is exactly what you are doing and he is so dumb that he is falling for it!"

"Shut your trap, both of you! You talk too much!" Said Hudba La, dusting himself off and leaping into the air to attack once more. He used all his power and increased it to its breaking point.

"This is my ultimate power and this is your end!" He screamed.

That was indeed the end of the fight. Discerner took the full force of the blow, and it connected like shattering earth underneath a tsunami. She fell on the ground with her armor crumbling in pieces and falling away from her, her clothes torn and tattered.

"I got you now." Said Hudba La, feeling confident in his ability. These would be his last words, however. In that moment, he tried to unleash his most powerful attack, but he did not notice that Discerner allowed him to land the blow on her to get full access to his body while he prepared for the final blow. Tumbling through the air, fully exposed and unaware, Hudba La ran straight for Discerner.

In a flash she was up, and she slammed her fiery fist into his abdomen, completely destroying him from the inside.

As he faded away into nothingness Judge sighed, saying, "I told you man, there is no stopping her when she gets like this. C 'mon tomato, let us go." Discerner was as red as a tomato from the flames coming out of her body. She replied, "Well, if that is the case, then I am not a tomato anymore, I think you should be calling me ketchup instead." And they both laughed.

"You see, you are not the only one cracking bad jokes at awkward moments."

Chapter 13

As the founders of Till Rest Save, the Snaitsirch group built their headquarters at the entrance of Till Rest Save. The fight between Discerner and the brothers was mere feet away from them and they heard word from the commotion that some fearless warriors were visiting the Kingdom, thrashing and defeating all their opponents on their way through the districts.

They were looking for the guardians of the Secret Relics. They were speechless when they heard these words. They knew the Holy Book was acting weird, but they did not know that it had called for help from the outside world.

"There are no coincidences, it must be them." They thought. "The ones the prophecy speaks about. There are no coincidences with God, but there are God-incidences. "We need to head there and intercept these two warriors and stop more bloodshed." The leader said. The Snaitsirch group are indeed the guardians of the Secret Relics, even though they did not know what they were guarding.

They had specific instructions to guard the relics in secret and only the guardian was to pass it from one guardian to the next. Not even the other members of the Snaitsirch group knew the location of these relics, they only knew they were guarding them. They thought that the Secret Relic was the Holy Book itself and nothing more, but they did not know the full story.

At the crowning of the first King and Queen of Till Rest Save, each of them received a sword. The sword given to King Yer Siul was in fact not an ordinary sword, it was the last element of the most powerful sword for the human race, and part of the fruit of the Spirit. It was the "*Longsuffering*" sword, or as they call it in the words of the humans "*Endurance.*" Even though the power of the sword is not effective in the spiritual Kingdom, its shadow gives the Kingdom the ability to endure all the hardships and to overcome them. They have been hiding this element from humanity, and as a result, humanity has been losing its patience and trying to overcome it, but with no success. They have not been able to endure the hardships of their lives and they are turning against one another in the human world.

There is still another treasure, or Holy Relic hiding in Till Rest Save. It is the other sword given to the first Queen of Till Rest Save, Anirefes. That is the sword containing the Gifts of Tongues. The hiding of this sword hindered humanity from speaking clearly with one another, leading them into chaos and confusion. The Gift of the Spirit has been hiding in plain sight, hijacked by spiritual forces who came from another world. But there is a deeper secret in Till Rest Save, which no one has ever thought about.

• • • • • • • ••

"Let us make a deal; no matter what happens, if we have to fight again, it will be my turn." Said Judge, pleading with Discerner.

"I agree with you, it is ok, you can take it. I guess your *tomato* cannot fight right way anyway."

"You mean my ketchup." And they both laughed.

"Stop making me laugh, it hurts to laugh!" Said Discerner. "Remember, we need to find the guardians in order to locate the treasures. It seems like no one in this Kingdom is aware of the Holy Relics or the secret treasure."

"Well, from what I have seen so far, I don't think they are hiding any secret treasures." And they both laughed.

"I told you Judge, stop cracking jokes. I am hurt."

• • • • • • • ••

Epop-Nabru and Epop-Suip were the proud protectors of Hont Well Kingdom and part of the head of the Scilohtac group. At the very center of Nede Land, the capital of the world.

To the people, they were very charismatic leaders and had much influence in their inner circle, but no one knew their secret life, the one they had been hiding for years.

In their secret chambers they were always devising plans to create their own ways or sects. There were many things they could not do right because the ones over them were blocking their way, but they were deep, revolutionary thinkers who were ready to bring change into a system that was old and stuck in the ancient ways.

They wanted to reform the system from within, not just change the aspects they thought were not good enough for the Scilohtac group. Before becoming part of the leaders in the group they were fighters, originally trained to fight at the Soultai Tournament, but their ways of thinking and acting led them down another path, the path of sanctification and solitude, according to them.

"I want to change this, but I am not that strong, spiritually speaking. I cannot continue hiding my true nature, for I fear I am going to burst one of these days. I love women and the fact that I cannot be with them or have them all around me

is my biggest challenge and temptation." Said
Epop-Nabru.

"Yes, this is our biggest challenge, we must
change this unjust system from within." Replied
Epop-Suip.

Years passed by and they were still controlling
their weaknesses, but one day, they saw two of the
most beautiful creatures they had seen in their
lives. These women were like angels to them, and
they were both immediately mesmerized by them.

"Look at that!" Shouted one of the brothers. "Look
who is coming this way again this week and try
not to show that you are looking. They must be
twin sisters, and we are here, alone, just listening
to them sharing their weaknesses and lustful
desires. They come here every single week, even
when they have their husbands with them. They
are only complaining that they do not satisfy
these goddesses of the universe."

They could not resist any longer, they came out of
their chambers where they had been listening to
them and invited them to have a more private talk,
so they could hear more of their needs and
weaknesses. After all, they just wanted to help
them.

"Are you feeling comfortable?" Asked Epop-Nadru,
and the women replied with a flirting smile that
yes, they were. Out of nowhere, Epop-Suip came

into the room holding a glass of wine for each of them. They unleashed their desires and devoured one another, and there was no feeling of guilt or remorse afterward.

This practice became a regular, weekly thing, and after several months of going through the same experience, a new feeling started to arise among them; the one they call "love."

"But we are already married, there is nothing we can do about it, we cannot end our marriage. Perhaps with your power you could do something about it though." Said the two women, tempting the emotions and feelings of these two fleshy, weak men.

They came up with a new law, giving unhappy women the right to leave their husbands, but only by strict approval of the hierarchy, and only after hearing the arguments of both parties. That law did not work well for Epop-Nadru and Epop-Suip, because even after this, they were not able to marry their new girls. Their creed forbade them to do so. As a result, they came up with a secret plan to poison the husbands and get rid of their bodies. The four of them were successful at the task, and they were able to marry with little suspicion. They lived happily in secret for years.

One day, King Rosuled discovered their wrong doing; he saw that they had created a new law for their own pleasure, and that they had committed adultery with married women. He also discovered that they had plotted to kill their husbands and get rid of the bodies, and on top of all this, they wanted to create their own group to follow them. There were many following their path already.

King Rosuled could forgive all the other crimes, but not the last one, and that is how these two mighty warriors who were part of the highest hierarchy at the capital were sent to a dumpster like Till Rest Save. He gave them two options, either die with their loved ones for their wicked behaviors, or be exiled forever in Till Rest Save Kingdom. The answer was obvious. Since they did not want to die, and since they were just beginning to taste their sinful nature and lustful desires, they felt they were not nearly done experiencing these feelings. They chose to be exiled to Till Rest Save Kingdom.

For Epop-Nadru and Epop-Suip, being sent to Till Rest Save was not a punishment at all, on the contrary, it was the perfect reward for them. They positioned themselves at the second zone of Till Rest Save, showing their strength and influence, and still collecting secret taxes from weaker beings, and most of all, cultivating their lustful desires in the open with no one to oppose them. Of course, their version of the story of why there were exiled is completely different; according to them they were sent as representatives of the Scilohtac group, by the King himself. They were not able to create their own version of Scilohtac and so they came to Till Rest Save.

There was only one small group opposing their ways of living, but they were too little and too weak to do more than speak against their behavior, and that was the *Snaitsirch group*. But everyone feared to touch anyone from the *Snaitsirch group*...they feared the curse.

Chapter 14

"We are now entering the grey zone." Said Judge because everything was in grey. That was the designated color for the people of Scilohtac.

"Watch out, the grey zone is approaching." Continued Judge, teasing Discerner. "Grey and red catchup are catching up." He said, giggling.

"Can you stop your silliness, please? Don't you see that I am hurt? All this laughing is not helping at all." Inquired Discerner.

"That is the idea, laughter is good for your health and for healing, or so they say."

They were not even done with their silly conversation when two men, dressed in robes approached them.

"Are you the ones stirring up our Kingdom and creating problems?" Asked Epop-Nadru in a very aggressive tone of voice.

"And who might you two be, the men in grey or something?" Asked Judge laughing.

"I see you have a good sense of humor, but it will not save you." Answered Epop-Suip. "Anyone disturbing our peace and way of living will pay dearly. It is time to pay your taxes, boy." Said Epop-Nadru. "We might keep the woman to ourselves, but you, we won't spare you." He continued.

"Judge, do you think you can put me down and deal with these two clowns or do you need me to fight?"

"No, it is ok, my little catchup." Said Judge to Discerner while laying her down to rest.

"I will fight him alone." Said Epop-Nadru to Epop-Suip, and Discerner yelled to them,

"I don't think that is such a good idea. If you want to survive, the two of you together have a greater chance of surviving. You see, he is not yet angry, but I could sense his heart, he is almost there and it looks like your comment about me is speeding up the process and you don't want to see him angry."

"Shut your mouth, silly woman, you are only good to mount!" When Judge heard this comment, he said.

"That is it! No more!" He lunged at both of them with lightning speed and grabbed their faces with his bare hands and thrashed them on the ground violently. Dirt and mud erupted from the ground and a fissure opened underneath them, such was the force Judge used to pummel them into the ground. While they were still on the ground, he started beating them up savagely. It was a surprise attack, and neither of the Epops where ready for this reaction.

When turning themselves over on the ground, they managed to stand up by launching a small attack on Judge, catching him off guard.

"I will not forgive you for this!" Both Epops shouted. Judge did not even bother to answer them and unleashed his second volley of attacks, hurting both of his rivals with one single blow.

"This is real, this guy is strong. We cannot lose to them!" And with that proclamation, the Epops combined their forces and slammed Judge into the ground with a powerful blow that split the ground apart for a hundred yards in every direction. A meteor strike couldn't have caused more damage.

"Now he is really angry." Said Discerner.

Standing up amid the debris and dust and showing them his full splendor, Judge was a fully transformed knight in a Purple-gold helmet, fit with purple diamond shield, a purple bronze breastplate, a purple silver belt and his purple Spartan sandals. Fire was emanating from all over his body and the flames from his sandals increased with every step toward his foes. What was more, Judge decided to use a fatal attack on Epop Nadru and Epop Suip.

Suddenly, from a short distance, Judge heard someone yelling, "Stop fighting, stop the fight, we are the ones you are looking for!" And when Judge turned his face to see who had shouted, he saw a couple of young men coming their way; he tried to stop his attack on the Epops, and he thought he did, but when he turned his gaze to where they had been, he realized it was too late for them. The battle was already over and they were no more. The immense power of Judge combined with the flames and his sword, reduced them to ashes.

• • • • • • • ••

"We came as soon as we heard the news of your battles. We tried to make it on time, but it looks like it is too late for them. We are the guardians of the secret relics." Said Sesom and Hajile.

"Everybody, to their households, we will take it from here. You two, come with us. Brother Hajile, attend to the wounds of the lady while I have a little chat with this man." Said brother Sesom.

"Why are you here and how did you get here?" Inquired Brother Sesom, taking Judge by the arm and hastily turning him away. Judge gave him all the details about their adventures on earth, about locating the Holy Book and how the Holy Book had pulled them to this new world.

"Our mission is to retrieve the Holy Relics and take them back home. We did not intend on fighting, but there was no other way for us to get here." Said Judge.

"I see," replied Sesom quizzically, "so the Holy Book was calling for help. It's no wonder we have been feeling an uneasy vibe coming out of the Holy Book lately." He walked with Judge, and continued.

"But why did the Holy Book not tele-transport you directly to our territory? The Snaitsirch territory is at the entrance of Till Rest Save, but you started right at the end."

"Well, it looked like the fight was inevitable and the Holy Book, as you mentioned, agreed with us. We did not ask to be here; we were brought here." Replied Judge.

. . ..

The Holy Book is the book forbidden by Scilohtac group. They barred the book from being read because they found people getting new knowledge from it, and some of them even surpassed the knowledge of the elders and defied them. The Chronicles of the True and Living God are found in the Holy Book as are all the adventures of the ancestors on Earth. Freedom and Salvation come to everyone who studies it and learns from it. Even though freedom and salvation are not manifested the same way as on Earth. In Nede Land, that freedom and salvation means something else. It means doing the right thing and following the right path. They were the ones holding the key to Earth and the entirety of humanity, having the book in the wrong hands would be the complete loss of humans, and total chaos and destruction would reign. The Holy Book needed to be kept safe from evil hands; thus, no one knew the true meaning of it.

• • • • • • • ••

"We don't know the location of the secret treasures or Holy Relics, we were left in charge of protecting the Holy Book, and because of this we've heard stories and we think we might have uncovered the location, but we are not sure, and we have not been allowed to access it. Only a human can have access to this place and reach for the Holy Relics." Said Sesom.

"There is an ancient book," he continued, "besides the Holy Book, but it was what the first King and Queen, Yer Siul and Anirefes left for the children to play with and for their parents to read. It contained stories of adventures and secret treasures that captivated the imagination of the children and gave the parents opportunities to spend more time with their children.

We all know the stories because they were our daily bread, and we have kept it this way, even though the books have vanished; we've kept the stories in our hearts and passed them from generation to generation as our forefathers instructed our people. Still, there is only one survivor from the time of the first King and Queen, and he is a very old man, but he is the one passing the stories to our children." Judge's eyes lit up when he heard this.

"We can take you to him and find out what he knows about the possible location of the Holy Relics from ancient times."

"I think we have a plan." Smiled Judge.

Chapter 15

The old man is blind and old; he said that it was his punishment for his sins, but no one knows what his sins were. Every adult calls him Nali, the children call him Nali, but we barely use his name since he is the oldest in all Till Rest Save. Everyone just calls him "old man."

When they went to the old man's house, there was no one there and the children explained that he was always sitting on the horizon as though expecting someone. When he is not telling stories to children, he is expecting "The one to come," as he says.

The children grabbed the hands of Judge and Sesom and took them to where the old man was sitting.

"Why are you here, Sesom, Hajile, I smelled you from a mile away, but I cannot discern the identities of the two who are with you. I take it they are not from this Kingdom. Come closer, dear, I want to see you." He said to Discerner in a low but commanding voice.

"See me? But he is blind, how will he see me?" Thought Discerner to herself.

"Come close, don't be afraid, I won't bite." He said with a laugh. "Oh! I see! A strong woman warrior! And you my dear, come closer." This time, he directed his words towards Judge. "I see! A very strong warrior." The old man seemed to discover many things about them by just palpating their faces.

"You are the strong warriors the children have been talking about, the ones defeating everyone on your path. And I guess you have come from Earth to claim the secret relics." He laughed.

"Yes, we have." Gasped the two warriors in unison.

"My dear, I regret to tell you that you are not the ones to retrieve them. Let me tell you a little story." He raised his face to the sky and breathed deeply before relating the tale to them.

"*One will rise from the horizon, coming from another world. He will bear the mark of royalty, the mark of Kings. He will not come along, his son will come and he will be greater than his father. When they arrive, the entire world of Nede Land will tremble. Only the blood of the heir and true King can carry the secret relics; only the worthy ones could pull them from their resting place. By blood they were hidden and by blood will they be revealed. This is where everything ends and where everything begins."*

• • • • • • • ••

"But no one knows except me, so I will take you to the place and give you the opportunity to retrieve them."

Astonished, Judge spoke, "Thank you very much Mr. Nal." Said he. "Very much obliged."

"It has been long time since I've heard the rest of my name." They did not mind nor pay any attention to his closing words, they just wanted to go and see for themselves the location of the relics. As he turned, the old man said, "Step back a little bit, please." There were two big trees next to him and when he opened his arms, the trees opened themselves at the base, revealing a sword inside each of them. But they were stuck to the ground.

"These are the swords of our King Yer Siul and Queen Anirefes, the first and only King and Queen of Till Rest Save." He said reverentially with a low bow.

"*They* are also the holy relics. The sword to your right is the sword of the King, also known as the Sword of Longsuffering or Endurance. I believe that is the way you say it in your world. The sword on your left is the sword of the Queen, also known as the Sword of Tongues or Gifts of Tongues, as you call it in your world. If you are the chosen ones and worthy, you may try to dig out the swords."

Without hesitation, Judge and Discerner went to withdraw the swords, but they were repelled immediately and were not even able to touch them.

"I don't understand, we came for these holy relics and we cannot even touch them. How is that possible?" Wondered Judge and Discerner.

"You might be confused," said the old man, seeing them lost in their thoughts and feeling powerless, " but you two were merely the channels to pave the way for the ones to come. You are not the chosen ones and that is clear. The chosen ones must be from the same bloodline, the royal bloodline. They will be father and son."

"But Nal, how is that possible? I think that particular prophecy is a little twisted because every single one with the blood of the King and Queen were wiped from this world." Added Sesom.

"I believe these holy relics will stay trapped within these trees for all eternity." Exclaimed Hajile, disappointed.

"If that were true, I would have died long ago," said the old man, "as it is part of my curse to see with my own eyes the return of the royal bloodline. On that day, I will surely die."

Seeing the sadness and disappointment in the eyes of the warriors, the old man placed his hand on Discerner's shoulder. "Do not be discouraged, you have paved the way for them to come, and now I am sure they will come and that the day is not far away."

After defeating all the enemies that were before them, Judge and Discerner gained the right to choose whoever was going to represent them as the head of Till Rest Save. They were the strongest and none of the other groups were able to oppose them.

On that day, they declared Sesom and Hajile the leaders and head of Till Rest Save and they also appointed Nal, "The old man" as advisor and councilor to the two new leaders of all Till Rest Save. Snaitsirch group was once more in command, and they upheld the task of sharing with everyone else the truth about the prophecies and the ones that were to come.

"We will return to Earth, but soon someone else will come to take our place!" Said Judge and Discerner, their last words in Till Rest Save Kingdom.

Chapter 16

*T*he *Emissary* had been praying, and training
his mind and body, because he knew it would not
be an easy task.

To access "*Hont Well Kingdom*" on the spiritual
plane, he needed to face the Guardian. He tried
twice, but failed. For many years since that time,
he studied many ancient texts and pondered their
meaning. Some had helped him, others profited
him almost nothing. In his prayers he asked God
to grant him insight, even though he knew that
God would grant him this insight in *His* own good
time, and not on account of his request. Rising
from the floor where he knelt, The Emissary
began preparing for bed.

He washed his face in the basin, the cool water
refreshing and relaxing him, and stood next to the
window to survey the glory of God's blessed
nighttime. On this night, the sky was empty, no
stars shining from the heavens. The Emissary, in
his room, heard a voice coming from the corridor,
and rose to investigate. It was the mysterious man,

known only as Kimura Ichi. Something was wrong.

"You've come a long way from that alley we found you in, my friend. You even chose a new name. Fitting, I think." Mused The Emissary.

The tall man just stood there, silently.

"What are you doing here, Kimura?"

"I…" He hesitated. "I have been hearing a voice calling to me, but it does not make sense." Replied Kimura. "The voice is calling me to *Hont Well Kingdom*. But isn't that the name of this town?" Kimura stepped closer to The Emissary. "So, why does the voice beckon me to a place I am already in?" He hissed.

The Emissary did not know how to answer. He was perplexed by the statement. "Kimura Ichi has been called." He thought. "What does it mean?"

The Emissary decided to take a chance. He sat down with Kimura and began explaining some of his past fights; battles of unparalleled devastation. He told Kimura that before they found him in the shadow of an alleyway, he was a fearless evil leader called "*Evil Sword*". Kimura could not believe what he was hearing, but somehow, miraculously, he started to remember the things The Emissary was telling him.

Slowly, Kimura spoke, "When I was back in the dark alley, eating from a dumpster, I could not think, and I did not know anything. Yet, somehow, I felt like something or *someone* was calling me. But at the same time, there were these strange creatures tormenting me and trying to devour me. When things were at their worst, that man showed up."

"Pastor Good." Confirmed The Emissary.

Kimura nodded. "I did not know who he was or what he wanted. Though I could not speak, or understand anything he was saying to me, I knew I had to follow him. They took me in, and from the minute I entered the building, I felt a warm presence, like nothing I had ever felt before. I felt good for the first time in what felt like forever. Then…" he began to tremble with emotion, "some of the people placed their hands on me and they spoke words I could not understand. At that moment, I saw a great light, shining and bright. There was a hand in the light and that hand grabbed me, and I heard a voice saying,

"*You are my child now. There is a purpose for you in my Kingdom*".

"My eyes were opened and I just said "*YES!*" to that voice." Kimura broke off and wiped a tear from his cheek.

"I understand that I was once an evil man, but no longer. I serve the Lord, God Almighty now."

"I know," said *The Emissary* "and that is why you are hearing the call from "*Hont Well Kingdom*". It is a call from a spiritual world and it looks like you have received free passage."

The Emissary explained everything, and Kimura Ichi, now aware of the situation, was ready to face anything that would come his way.

In spite of this, *The Emissary* questioned himself. *He'd* never received free passage. In fact, he'd lost in battle against the Guardian in his town several times. But he decided that he was ready to face the challenge once again, and he and Kimura set off for the Secret Entrance.

Once they reached the Secret Entrance, they found the Guardian standing in front of it, poised and ready for battle. Curiously, when the Guardian saw Kimura Ichi, he immediately bowed and acknowledged him, saying in a menacing voice,

"*You have been granted safe passage*, but only you." The Guardian gestured to Kimura.

"But, is not time for you to enter."

"Not time?" Said Kimura.

"The Emissary must defeat me, or be defeated himself. Only *then* will I open the gate. Yet, a single person cannot pass through the gate alone; there must be two, even though they may face different challenges."

Straightening his back and breathing deeply, The Emissary turned to Kimura Ichi.

"Do not intervene."

"But I..." Kimura started.

The Emissary interrupted. "Whatever happens, do not interfere with this battle. It is mine."

As the last syllable passed The Emmisary's lips, the Guardian rushed him with terrifying speed, swinging at his head. Emissary, ducking the blow by millimeters, recovered himself and engaged the Guardian head on.

A fierce battle ensued, and though it was taxing on him, The Emissary had no intention of losing this battle, not this time. He was more determined than ever. He felt a stabbing pain in his right leg. It was the tip of the Guardian's sword, sinking into his flesh.

"I have you now," said the Guardian, withdrawing his sword and swinging for The Emissary's head once again.

Suddenly, out of nowhere, The Emissary shouted in a mighty voice, "Heavenly Rain!"

These words seemed to infuse The Emissary's bright sword with an immense power, and he struck a critical blow against the Guardian, shattering his armor.

"How?" The Guardian gurgled, watching blood spill from his leg as he struggled to move it.

"I don't believe it." The Guardian exclaimed. He was trying to gather his thoughts and grasp the reality of the situation.

The Emissary decided to interrupt his thinking to share some information.

"You see, in all our previous fights; the fights I lost to you; I never learned the key to defeating you. You hurt me, badly, and I lost over and over and over again. I lost because I was not ready to give everything I had to this battle, and release my most powerful attack against you. I always held back. But this time," The Emissary stepped closer to the Guardian, "it was all or nothing. Not many can survive my heavenly sword technique. I'm impressed that you're only bleeding from your leg."

Smiling, the Guardian spoke. "You have finally defeated me. You did not defeat me in the past because this is a fight for your very life, and if you don't put your whole self into a fight like that, you will never win. I am glad I was able to see your attack and block it before losing my head. Though my sword is broken, I can replace it."

The Guardian stood with an effort, "Congratulations! Many challenges await you, and there is still much for you to learn. You two will hear the call for your entrance soon. In the meantime, you must prepare, whatever is coming, it will not be as easy to deal with as I was." With that, the Guardian vanished.

From that moment on, The Emissary and Kimura Ichi were waiting for the call to enter the new Kingdom.

"I think we have been waiting too long." Said the Emissary to Kimura. "Let us start a BPF first thing in the morning."

"You mean Bible, Praying and Fasting?" Reaffirmed Kimura.

"Yes, that is indeed what I am referring to. Let us meet at 5:55 am tomorrow morning."

The next morning, they were reading the Bible, Praying and Fasting when suddenly...

"Do you hear the bells? I did not even know that we had bells in the church." Mentioned Kimura.

"No, I don't hear a thing." Replied The Emissary.

The bells rang a second time, and a third time. The Emissary was able to hear them this time, however, and they both said, "It is time." And at that moment their spiritual eyes were opened, and a very bright light seemed to be approaching them. They heard a sound of a big gate creaking, or so they thought, and they were engulfed by the light.

• • • • • • • • • • • •••

Hont Well is the greatest Kingdom in all of Nede Land. It is completely surrounded by water, which acts as a natural barrier on all sides. There are mountains and vast walls of trees, and large species of vegetation as well. It appears as an island in the middle of a circular mountain range.

The citizens of Hont Well Kingdom believe themselves to be at the pinnacle of all civilizations. They are the type of people that adore and respect all the saints and prophets. They respect and accept the beliefs of all other Kingdoms, which is one of their most important and respectable characteristics. They are, after all, the leaders of all the Kingdoms.

The river that surrounds the Kingdom of Hont Well pours into four different outlets at the cardinal directions, each forming a riverhead that becomes a river in itself and nourishes one of the other four Kingdoms in Nede Land.

At each riverhead, there is a watchtower which holds a gate into the city, and in each watchtower, there is a Guardian keeping that gate at all times. To enter the Kingdom, one must be granted passage by the Guardian in the first tower, named *Posin*. After receiving his blessing, you must travel to each of the remaining three towers

(*Hogin, Kelddehi and Teseuphra*) and obtain passage from each of the Guardians.

Each Guardian is independent from one another. Having safe passage from one of the towers does not guarantee safe passage from the others. After passing the fourth tower (*Teseuphra*), you will see a massive open gate leading to the Great Hall which stretches from one end of the Kingdom to the other.

In the middle of the hall, there is a tremendous fountain that towers into the cloudy canopy of the mountains, high above the earth. When viewed from below, the ceiling of the Great Hall appears to be the blue mantle of the sky itself. All the clouds at the zenith of that great expanse converge in the center and fall as rain into the torrent of the fountain, which then feeds the waters of the Four Kingdoms in outpourings from its well. Some say that Hont Well Kingdom holds the most terrible and amazing secret in all of Nede Land.

To its citizens, Hont Well is something of a mystery. Its ubiquitous water sources, giving rise to gargantuan vegetation, and its sprawling mountain ranges make the Kingdom of Hont

Well an intimidating frontier. Though the citizens are all unusually friendly, it is foolish to mistake their gentle demeanor for weakness. They are among the most powerful beings in Nede Land, and oversee the Four Kingdoms.

Men of this Kingdom are extremely handsome and powerful, and bring honor to the land. They believe that their waters generate an incredible vibration in the bodies of their men, making them the most exuberant and vivacious of all warriors.

The women in the Kingdom are naturally the most fair and beautiful in Nede Land. They possess wisdom and strength beyond comparison, and their charms are subtle and alluring. There is a Governor appointed to supervise the tributes and bureaucracies of all the Kingdoms in Nede Land. Her name is Lebezej, and she is a fearless, strong and beautiful woman. People say that she visited each of the Four Kingdoms a single time, long ago. But that was all that was required to inspire the people to pay her homage as Governor. Only the King is above her, and even the Guardians, who fear her, are her subjects. Occasionally she sends her most-trusted servant, Laab, to supervise the Kingdoms, acting as her eyes and ears.

Laab is a "prince charming," of sorts, and he likes to drink and look for fights whenever he can, being *intimately* aware of his own strength and skills. Yet, of all the indulgences he finds pleasure in, it is women that he adores the most. He is loved by all young women. And what's not to love? He is charming and cavalier, a true romantic.

Ironically, Laab trained his master, Lebezej, in the art of combat. They grew up together, and he took her under his care. Being a little older than her, Laab taught her everything she knows about fighting and endowed her with great wisdom. In all the Kingdoms, Laab and Lebezej are the most popular and famous names. Not even the King himself compares in sheer popularity.

Rosuled, the King of Hont Well Kingdom, is a very charismatic ruler. All the other Kingdoms are subject to him and pledge their allegiance to *Rosuled.* The other Kingdoms pay tribute to him and his people, providing for all they could ever need. But, being the richest Kingdom in Nede Land enables the King to be very generous, and he always acknowledges those worthy of recognition.

Once a year, King Rosuled hosts a marvelous festival which citizens from all five Kingdoms look forward to and enjoy. At this festival, all the other Kings pay their annual tributes and participate in the games. The festival lasts ten days, and each day, every Kingdom can present two of its best fighters to compete in the Grand Tournament, or Soultai Tournament. There is one battle per day, the losers are eliminated, and the winners progress to the next round.

There are five rounds in the tournament. The first round lasts for five days, and all ten fighters compete, and the winners proceed to the next round. Round two lasts two days, and four of the five fighters demonstrate their skills and eliminate their opponents. The third round lasts one day only, and, in it, two of the three remaining fighters demonstrate their skills, leaving only one standing in the end. In the fourth round, which also lasts for a single day, the last two opponents face each other, and the winner of the tournament becomes the rightful challenger of the champion who won the previous year's tournament, who is now a citizen of Hont Well Kingdom and the protégé of King Rosuled.

The fifth and final day of the tournament is either a great fight between the previous champion and the contender, for the ultimate title "*Champion of Champions*," or a celebration welcoming the winner of the tournament as part of King Rosuled's Elite Guard instead. If this is his choice, he receives the finest training in all the styles of the Five Kingdoms, making him worthy to be counted among the best of Nede Land's fighters.

There are many other benefits to winning the tournament. Not only does the winner get to decide between challenging Hont Well's champion, or joining Rosuled's Elite Guards, he also gets to live in abundance and splendor, with immense wealth at his disposal.

The Kingdom where the winner of the tournament resides gets the opportunity to demand a chance at the throne of Hont Well Kingdom, by claiming the right of *the challenger*, which is the only right that the King of Hont Well Kingdom cannot refuse. Refusing or neglecting the claim the challenger means stepping down from the throne and the public declaration that the current King cannot defeat his challenger; and for the most powerful Kingdom in all Nede Land, that is not an option. They must always have the most powerful King. In the history of Nede Land, nobody has ever claimed this right.

All other Kingdoms believe that there is only one worthy enough to claim this right, and it is the King Babul–Ell. Many citizens wonder why the almighty King Babul–Ell has never claimed this right, even after winning many tournaments. There is no clear explanation why he has never tried to do it. To claim the right of *the challenger*, the challenging Kingdom must first prove that its fighter is worthy enough to fight King Rosuled. The challenging Kingdom's fighter must first defeat Rosuled's appointed fighter, proving his right to fight the King.

Chapter 17

The pinnacle of the world, the supreme race and the capital of *Nede Land*.

Some think that Hont Well is the closest city to heaven and that its men are the closest to God. That is what others think, and it is how Hont Well wants to be seen.

They have been ruling since the beginning of time and they will continue to rule the whole of Nede Land for ages yet to come. They are the most cunning and intelligent men of all. They show themselves as sheep when in reality they are the wolves; the predators of Nede Land. They are the source of everything, and they are placed at the head of all Kingdoms.

Legend says that Hont Well was the first Kingdom established in all Nede Land, then came all the other Kingdom. Some even say that the pinnacle of the word was created by the gods themselves and that is why Hont Well was the first in the line of Kingdoms with buried treasures and secrets not known to anyone in Nede Land.

The secrets will reveal themselves when the time comes. Meanwhile, King Rosuled is the head of all Nede Land and King of Hont Well, the main source for all Nede Land.

They have the power to shut off water supplies to all Kingdoms. Since Hont Well is a Kingdom surrounded by water, it creates each river which waters the entire land. Posin, Hogin, Kelddehi and Teseuphra are the heads of the rivers that originate in Hont Well.

King Rosuled is always keeping a low profile in the Kingdom, since there are other figures more popular than the King. Two of such are Lebezej and Laab. They supervise all the other Kingdoms and collect taxes from them. Even when Lebezej does not collect them in person, she has her ways or systems that she uses to collect them, increasing the richness of Hont Well.

"Your sanctity, the seal to and from earth has been broken and we may have guests shortly." Said Tseirp, the Advisor to the King. "I fear that the guardian has been defeated or he has given free entrance to the Kingdom for reasons I cannot fathom and I cannot advise you on the matter, your highness."

"I will have words with the guardian about it. Summon Tobba immediately and let us see what he has to say about this breach."

After a short while, Tobba appeared in the presence of the King.

"My lord, I am here. How can I serve you?"

The King leaned forward on his throne ominously. "When were you planning to inform me that you deliberately allowed humans into my Kingdom? Did you think that I would not know what is going on in my own Kingdom?"

"Your highness," bowed Tobba, "you were the one giving me instructions on whom to allow into the Kingdom; those that are worthy to find the Holy Relics, those you are looking for." Replied Tobba.

"Ah! Very Well." The King threw his hands in the air in jubilation. "Please proceed and keep me informed." Said King Rosuled.

"But my Lord, they are intruders and we cannot allow anyone to come into our Kingdom." Protested Tseirp.

"Are you trying to contradict my words?" Asked the King inquisitively.

"No no, your highness." Responded Tseirp, meekly. "Please accept my apologies."

"Leave me now!" Shouted the King.

Even though he is the King of Hont Well, there are many things that he does not know or that he has not discovered, because he is not one of the chosen ones. He has been looking for them for decades with no success at all.

"Will these guests be my salvation? I have been searching for it for ages and I still cannot find the secret entrance. I must put my fate in the ultimate power of them all, but no one should know about it or I will have problems." Reflected King Rosuled to himself.

• • • • • • • ••

Tnias Suinac was a brave and strong warrior, worthy of the gate of Teseuphra River facing Mock Fenk Fist Kingdom. His eyes were sharp and he could see everything in the past that related to his gate, though, he cannot see the future, but his knowledge of the past allows him to predict certain events.

According to legend, Tnias Suinac was one of the first champions that came out of Soultai. People don't speak much about it, since it was in ancient times, but the ancient chronicles describe that tournament as one of the most cruel and bloody of all time, because of Tnias Suinac.

In this first fight, with just his bare fists and a single punch, he was able to disfigure the face of his opponent into something beyond description, and that was the end of that.

In the second round, he used his mighty kick and thrashed his opponent with one single blow, making him look like a human elastic band, because he was left unrecognizable and his body was shattered.

In the third round, he used his sword, jumping through the air with a mighty blow and his opponent was split in two.

In the fourth round he used a combination of all his skills in a single attack, and his opponent was cast into oblivion.

It is said that he challenged the champion for the title of "Champion of Champions" the night before the battle. Tnias Suinac was transferred directly to the watchtower by the King himself, giving him the highest honor in all the Kingdom. He assumed the title of Guardian of Teseuphra Door and Seer of the Past.

Tnias Suinac has wondered what would have happened if he would have been given the opportunity to fight that battle, but the King promised him an even greater battle if he accepted the guardianship and he accepted the challenge. He was placed at the first gate to access the Kingdom, being given the honor to grant access to the other gates or not.

When he saw the gate opened, he knew something or someone strong was coming. He noticed that whoever it was; he was not coming from Mock Fenk Fist Kingdom, and according to the battles he saw, he was excited to see a rival as strong as the ones that fought at Mock Fenk Fist Kingdom. He studied each one of the movements displayed by these two warriors that defeated the Kingdom of Mock Fenk Fist. He had been almost certain that they would come, but he had not known who they would be.

"This shining light must be from earth, the one the King spoke about and the one I have been waiting for. They are humans and humans cannot even *enter* my Kingdom, much less defeat me."

Thought Tnias Suinac as two warriors appeared standing in front of him.

"Welcome to Teseuphra Door, I am the guardian. What has brought you to my Kingdom and what is your purpose?" He Inquired. Even though he knew what they were looking for, he was testing their honesty.

"Well, my friend, to be honest, we have been called here and we did not come in peace." Said The Emissary, sternly. "In fact, we came to take back what is rightfully ours."

"I assume you are prepared to fight. You look immensely strong, but that does not change the outcome. We are on a mission from *God Almighty* and you are standing in our way."

"I see!" Exclaimed the guardian. "I just wanted to confirm that you were honest and ready to face your end."

At that moment, Kimura Ichi stepped forward and said "Can I fight him?" Asking permission from The Emissary. "I have never fought a real battle, at least not since changing sides, so I would like to test a few theories."

"There is no objection from me, be my guest." Replied The Emissary.

The strong and tall man, aged but solid, took of his t-shirt by ripping it to shreds and kicked his sandals away into the dirt. He then placed his sword gently on his sandals.

"Ha! I see, you are planning to play a little bit before getting serious." Said Tnias Suinac. "That is good; let met me assess your strength then."

The fight began at an incredible speed. Kimura was testing his strength; he had fought many battles in the past but on the wrong side, this time he found himself fighting his first battle for the right side.

The combinations of kickboxing moves were too strong for Kimura, and he was having a hard time keeping up the pace with Tnias Suinac. Suddenly he received a jab on his face, sending him to the ground.

"Are you done testing, or do you want to test more?" Inquired Tnias Suinac.

"Not so fast, this is only the first round; let us go for the second round." Said Kimura, wiping the blood from his lips. This time it was Tnias Suinac that began to have problems keeping up with Kimura's blows. "This is a completely different man than before. He is very strong; he is almost stronger than my current level." Thought Tnias Suinac.

Suddenly, he bit the dust and started bleeding. Seeing his blood for the first time in ages made

Tnias Suinac remember his past battles and instead of getting angry, he felt happier.

"Ready for a round trip?" Said Tnias Suinac as he lunged with an incredible speed and strength, throwing punches and kicking like he was having a blast. His laugh was scarier than his blows.

He was actually having the time of his life, and out of nowhere Kimura was stricken to the ground. But Tnias Suinac did not stop, he could not control himself and continued beating Kimura. During the beating, Kimura began to bleed on the ground, and eventually lay motionless as though he were dead.

"Are you done, old man? Don't tell me you are dying on me so soon when I am having so much fun." Said Tnias Suinac, mockingly.

After a few minutes of kicking, he managed to restrain himself; he was getting tired after all and stepped back a little. "Oh man! I thought I killed him too soon. What about you standing over there, are you ready to fight?" Addressing his words to The Emissary.

"I don't think you should worry about me yet. Your opponent is behind you." He replied with a gesture toward Kimura. Tnias Suinac thought Kimaru was dead, but when he turned around, there he was standing tall, all beaten up and bleeding. Kimura used his hands to clean the blood from his mouth and face and then said, "It is time to get serious."

"Interesting! That's what I am talking about!" Shouted Tnias Suinac.

Though Kimura was called to serve the Lord, he still hadn't received a new name or transformation. He was fighting with his brute strength alone, and it was one of a kind.

Kimura started feeling new energy coursing through his body, like an electric flow filling him up and accelerating his heart. His pulse was so rapid that he had to start fighting, as though he were compelled. There was something like steam or smoke coming out of his body, like a glittering fog. Kimura was on fire and fighting like no other.

"I knew he is strong, that he was one of the strongest among evil commanders, but I did not know he was that strong. What a beast!" Thought the Emissary.

Suddenly, Kimura's blows became so strong that he was pressing down Tnias Suinac with every strike, forcing him down until he reached the ground. Kimura Said, "Stand up. I am not going to beat you while you're on the ground; stand up and fight, show me what you got!"

Tnias Suinac saw the battle of Mock Fenk Fist, but this was on another level. His nostalgia of fighting the champion and becoming the champion of champions was no longer comforting or exhilarating. Somehow, in the middle of the fight, his wish came true and all he wanted to do was bring his opponent down.

"No one has been able to stand in front of me after receiving the blows that you have, I will give you that. You are very strong," said Tnias Suinac, "but still, that is all you are and your strength does not compare to mine. I will show you my true strength!"

Increasing his power level to its maximum, Tnias Suinac did not show his full strength. With a single blow he sent Kimura away flying; the blow was so strong that the Emissary was dragged away by the whirlwind as well. Tnias Suinac drew his sword, his skills with which were unique in the Kingdom of Hont Well.

"Don't you die just yet!" He yelled, as the power from his blow cleared the fog, and he saw Kimura standing in the distance, now using his sword as well.

"I am no longer Evil Sword, my name is *Lightning Sword*!" Shouted Kimura while raising his sword and swinging it at Tnias Suinac. The guardian was now bleeding profusely from his right arm, but he was able to block the second blow.

"When did he get this new name? I did not know the Lord had changed his name; everything is happening so fast with this man." Thought the Emissary.

"I believe it is time to end this fight, don't you think?" Grinned Kimura.

"Yes, I will give you my ultimate and fatal blow as my next move. No one has ever survived this move, so consider yourself honored to die by my hand!" Said Tnias Suinac.

"Don't get so full of yourself, I am not going to show you my full strength; in fact, the attack that will extinguish you is not even my most powerful attack." Replied Kimura, raising his blade to meet his opponent.

"Oh man! That is so mean." Thought the Emissary. "How can he even say these words to such a strong opponent? There is no way that he could get stronger than this."

Kimura was now holding his sword with both hands. He said "Ikusu" meaning "Here I go," and at that moment there was a clash of titans; the swords met in the air and the sound of the swords resounded like a thousand voices screaming, and then all at once there was complete silence. Tnias Suinac was standing with his broken sword still in his hand and Kimura was lying on the ground still clutching his sword.

"Well done, old man." Said Tnias Suinac. "I am grateful for this fight, you can pass on now." With this he fell to the ground while Kimura got to his feet with the help of his sword. Tnias Suinac was defeated by the Lightning Sword. Mock Fenk Fist town and its guardian, were down.

When the news came to King Rosuled that the last tower had been defeated, he got very angry and gave strict instructions to each of the remaining guardians to stop the intruders at any cost; allowing them to access the Kingdom would surely earn them a torturous punishment.

• • • • • • • ••

"He finally found the fight he was looking for. I am sure he died happily after all." Thought Tnias Sutama, guardian of the Kelddehi tower, the next tower in line to meet these mighty people that have defeated a guardian.

There was once a man who went to participate in the Soultai Tournament. He was from a very small village in one of the Kingdoms, so small that no one thought a fighter would ever come out of it.

A young couple, each from a different Kingdom, got together and procreated. They named him Sutama. He was a lovely and charming child, very smart and quick to learn any craft. When his father saw how skillful the child was, he sent him to another Kingdom and asked a nameless warrior to train the child in the arts of fighting.

Sutama then learned the arts of fighting and passed from one master to another until he became a fearful and mighty warrior. He was taken to two Kingdoms and each Kingdom wanted him to be their fighter. His father was proud that other Kingdoms were trying to recruit his son, but Sultama did not have these Kingdoms in mind. He wanted to bring honor and glory to his father and the little village by fighting at the Soultai Tournament.

He won all preliminary matches from both Kingdoms and since no one was able to defeat him, he said that he was going to represent himself and his father at the Soultai Tournament. He was not going to give any glory to anyone but his father, as no kingdom deserved his gratitude.

His fierce and fearful way of fighting made him notorious among all the fighters of all the Kingdoms, and there was no one to match his strength. Legend says that when he went to participate in the Soultai Tournament, in every single fight he did not even have to raise his hand to defeat his opponent.

After merely witnessing his overwhelming presence and power, his enemies declared him the winner. He immediately became the challenger for the title "Champion of Champions." The only warrior to withstand his presence was Silativ. It was said that their strength was equally matched. They tried looking for a weak point on each other for over twenty minutes without moving a single finger.

They knew that either one of them only needed one single blow to end the fight. After a long wait, people started complaining, but when Sutama yelled for silence, the entire arena was compelled to stillness without even being able to move. That day King Rosuled made both fighters guardians of his Kingdom.

Chapter 18

Only a few chosen ones were able to obtain the title of Tnias; that was a title above all the others, earned with pure strength and sacrifice. The only one able to bestow such a title is King Rosuled. It is said that only four people in all the history of Hont Well Kingdom have earned the right to carry the title of "Tnias" and they are the fearless guardians of the towers at Hont Well Kingdom.

. . . .

"The guardians are fighting and one of them has been defeated, they say. The intruders must be strong that they can defeat a guardian; no one has ever done something like that. We fear for the fate of the Kingdom."

"There is no need to fear, if they manage to pass through the guardians, which I doubt, they will need to face Laab and Lebezej and on top of them, there are the guardians of the secret chamber." The unknown warriors that nobody has ever seen commented to another concerned citizen.

Hont Well is a Kingdom full of secrets, some that the citizens don't even know exist. Their King Rosuled has been stealing most of the power from humanity and hiding it in his secret treasure chamber, but there are other treasures he has been hunting down and searching for over the ages. He is still awaiting those who will show him the way to find them.

● ● ●● ● ●● ● ●●

"I see your power growing exponentially, congratulations," said the Emissary, "you are a powerful ally, and I am glad to have you on my side. Congratulations for your hero name, by the way; I did not know you had one… Lightning Sword." Reflected the Emissary, and they both laughed.

"There is something I still don't understand. We all have hero names that have meaning derived from the Holy Book, but your name I am not sure of, and I cannot picture its relationship with the Holy Book. But I am sure I will find out soon." He continued saying.

"I can understand why Shrewder and Faith Woman had a hard time defeating you back in the days at Blue Ball. I only heard the stories and thought they were joking, but now I see how powerful you are. Now, let us move on and get to the next tower; with you by my side I don't even have to fight!" Laughed the Emissary, jokingly.

"Wait! Now that I think about it, I have never seen you fight, and I don't even know how powerful *you* are." Said Kimura, now known as Lightning Sword.

When they arrived at the next tower, the tower of Kelddehi facing Newt Kingdom, they found this powerful guardian at the gate."

"State your name and your business, or perish."
The guardian paused and looked down
thoughtfully.

"But now that I think about it, there is no need for
that; I've already heard you are the enemy!" He
jumped down off his gate with a mighty blow and
attacked the Emissary full on. Kimura was able to
dodge the blow and stepped back, but the
Emissary met the guardian's sword with his bare
hand, blocking the strike unaided.

"Not so fast." Said the Emissary to the guardian
with a grin, peering out from behind the sword.
"At least let us know your name." The guardian
thrust once again, but with more strength this
time. The Emissary blocked it yet again.

"Barehanded? I did not know you were so strong."
Mentioned Lightning Sword. "You are not even
using your sword and you are able to block the
strikes from the guardian. I can sense the power
of the guardian, but I cannot sense any power
coming from you." He continued saying,
quizzically.

"Hey my friend! Guardian! My name is The
Emissary, and I am not the one to fight you today.
This one next to me will be your opponent."

"Nice to meet you! I am Tnias Sutama and I want
to fight you first. You don't look that strong, but
you've blocked my blows, so I want to see the

kinds of tricks you are hiding. I am sure you will not last much longer! Once I deal with you, I will end the life of your partner." Replied Tnias Sumata.

"Well, I think he does not want to fight me," said Lightning Sword, "he shows no interest in me, he wants you, Emissary. You will need to deal with him. Besides, I also want to see the tricks you are using." Commented Lightning Sword.

"What a partner you are! I was counting on you and you send me to the den of lions. Anyways, since you insist," now facing Tnias Sutama, "I will grant your wish, but I am curious about something." Said The Emissary.

The other guy my partner defeated was also called Tnias, are you two related or something?"

"Don't you worry about it. I will show you right now." The guardian got ready to charge The Emissary with a powerful blow...

"Wait! Wait! Wait! Hold on minute, not so fast. Looking like an old man, he took his shoes off and placed his shirt upon them. Now, only wearing a T-shirt, he said "I don't want to dirty my shirt."

"Are you serious, man?" Asked Lightning Sword.

"Yes, it was a precious gift from my dear friend, Warrior, and I only wear it on special occasions. Besides, I love this shirt." He said.

"Let us proceed now!" Suddenly the Emissary charged against Tnias Sutama with a strong kick, which put him on his knees, but at the very same moment he used his other leg and landed an incredible blow to the ribs of his enemy. You could hear the cracking sound from a distance, and a loud cry came out of Tnias Sutama in pain.

"You bloody rascal, how dare..." But the Emissary was not finished; he flew with his third blow, this time combining his kick with boxing which sent the guardian to the ground. While the guardian was on the ground, the Emissary got on top of him and began beating him badly. When he saw no movement from the guardian, he stood up.

"Is it over?" Asked Lightning Sword.

"Nope, just giving him a little time to recover his strength." Said the Emissary.

"You were saying about defeating me?" Asked the Emissary of Tnias Sutama.

"I can see you are incredibly strong, I misjudged you; but that won't happen again. I am ready now." Replied the guardian, returning to his feet.

"Good, I am glad to hear it. That is what I was waiting for." Replied the Emissary.

Charging at the guardian, the Emissary put the guardian down in the dust once again, but this time, the guardian laid a blow on the Emissary's jaw, causing blood to gush from his mouth.

"Allow me to show you the way I get when I know I am getting into an interesting battle. I normally don't do it, but I will make an exception for you." Said Tnias Sutama. At this moment, the two men felt an overwhelming presence coming out of Tnias Sutama.

"This is why only a few selected ones are called Tnias, because of our gigantic power. Rivals feel us and kneel before us when we share our true power, and I am not even using my full strength!" Laughed the guardian.

"Well, well, well! What do we have here? It looks like we have a dichotomy!" As he said this, the Emissary unleashed his power, and it was even stronger than the guardian's.

"As you can see, I did not want to get to this point, but you are making me reveal my strength to my partner." At that very same moment, the two warriors clashed with their fists, striking the very sky with their blows, and it seemed like they were dancing instead of fighting; their speed and agility were too fast for the untrained eye to follow, but not for Lightning Sword.

"You cannot be stronger than me, you are a mere human, and you can never surpass my strength!" Screamed the guardian while striking with furious force, throwing the Emissary on the ground like a ragdoll. "Why aren't you defending yourself? Why aren't you fighting back?" Yelled the guardian, getting infuriated by the Emissary's petulance. He was getting tired, but his opponent was bleeding and he sent him back on the ground. "Why!?" Slam. "Why!?" SLAM. "Why?!"

"I will answer your question!" The Emissary shouted, rebounding and recovering himself. "You think that because I am human, I am weaker than you. If you think so, you are completely mistaken. We are the only creatures able to evolve and increase our strength to unimaginable levels, because our strength does not come from the outside, our strength comes from within us, from the hero within us. The human race is the only race capable of hosting the Almighty Creator of the Universe. We are the only race in all the cosmos, on all the planets in all universes, realms and worlds that can host this power within us! Allow me to show you what I mean." Said the Emissary in a commanding voice while reaching out to grasp his sword. This time he said, "Heavenly Rain!" and his sword multiplied itself and fell as rain descending from heaven. The guardian was able to dodge most of the swords from the attack, but two of them were able to pierce both of his legs.

Tnias Sutama put his sword on the ground, grabbed the two piercing swords and pulled them out of his legs at the same time.

"You are a formidable foe," said the guardian, "but this does not change anything; I will now show you my full strength. I have never unleashed it before, you are the first one to experience it."

Lightning Sword was just watching the fight and learning all he could from his enemy, delighting himself at the same time while watching his buddy fight.

"Impressive power," said the Emissary, "and overwhelming as well. I am honored to see your full strength. Can you increase it a little bit more though?" Inquired the Emissary, teasing him. Now, Lightning Sword was having a hard time staying put and watching the fight because of the display of power. At this moment, the Emissary incrementally began raising his power, but his power was not yet up to the guardian's level.

"I see you are stronger than me, at least that is what you think." Said the Emissary. Then, for the first time, his Spartan sandals became visible, alight with flames and a substance that looked blue and pink at the same time. Right after that his blue-pink and silver belt appeared around his waist, and his strength was undetectable. In fact, neither Tnias Sutama nor Lightning Sword could read his strength level at all.

He disappeared with a flash, and a thunderclap accompanied his first strike against the guardian in this new form. The guardian managed to stand, but was met with yet another devastating blow to the midsection which sent him crashing to the ground once more. Standing, shakily, trying to block the Emissary's attack with his sword, he was met with an astounding blow that shattered his blade and pierced his body. The Emissary reappeared.

"As I said before, you are mistaken about our humanity; it is not our weakness but our strength." This incredible and powerful warrior was standing beside the guardian as a cloud of vibrating energy. The Emissary dealt one final blow against the guardian's helmed head, and, with what looked like a smirk, the guardian drew his last breath, and was no more.

Lightning Swords could not believe his eyes. The display of power from the Emissary was unbelievable.

"What were those sandals about? And that belt you had in the fight?" Inquired Lightning Sword.

"Those are part of my knightly armor." He said.

"Wait a minute! You are telling me that it was just part of your armor and your strength increased exponentially as a result? You are telling me that *that* display of power was not your full strength, and that you still got some more power hidden in there? Man! You sure are strong. I am glad to have a partner like you." He exclaimed in astonishment.

"Hold on!" He paused. "Will I get a suit of knight's armor too?" He asked, desperately.

"I don't know; I think you will, but it is not up to us, it is up the our Lord to give such things to you…or not. And once He gives it to you, He does not take it away, but I am not sure about you, you are strong enough now. I cannot imagine your strength with a set of armor." Replied the Emissary.

Chapter 19

"When our King, the King of Kings, calls us, He gives us a new name, and thus changes our old nature. Most people don't know about it, but when they are called, they become a new creature and their names are changed, but only those called to battle get to be made aware of their names.

It is not just the change in your name, it is the seal of the King, Yeshua, the True and Only King, that He gives His people. By this, he declares that this person belongs to Him and that he is not the same as he was before. That person is no longer bound to their evil and sinful nature." Said the Emissary.

"What about the armor?" Inquired Lightning Sword.

"Only true warriors who are ready to fight and are called to fight spiritual battles in realms like this one get to have the incredible power of the armor, but there are many hidden secrets in the armor that I still don't understand and cannot explain to you presently. We are about to walk to our next battle and we still don't know what awaits us in the third tour. So far, we have defeated them, and I'm not saying that it was easy, but I was expecting a little bit more from this Kingdom." And they both laughed.

• • • • • • • • •

The walk from Kelddehi tower was longer than expected. "I was hoping to have reached next gate already." Said the Emissary. "It seems like we have been walking for more than twenty minutes and we still haven't reached it."

"Yes, I don't understand it either, but something strange is happening. Are we moving in slow motion?" Asked Lightning Sword.

"I cannot answer that for certain, but I would agree with you on that one. We definitely need to figure out what is going on."

The guardian of Hogin tower had accumulated certain abilities over the years, and one of them was being able to create an illusion of movement. People would think that they were moving, but instead, they were standing still. Only a wise and sharp mind could perceive and avoid the trap.

That was one of the techniques he used to ward off unpleasant guests who dared to come to his tower, most of which were people who, after walking for 25 minutes or so in their minds, would give up and turn back. After all, the illusion could only be created for 35 minutes maximum, and only once in a long while.

Tnias Silativ was able to see some of the action in Kelddehi town with his special sightseeing and he knew these two approaching him now were trouble. He was not inclined to face trouble at this unpleasant time, but his two new guests were not going anywhere, and after the illusion disappeared, they were able to reach the gate. When they looked back it seemed impossible that they could have walked that distance in a very short time, they thought.

Turning to the guardian, the Emissary said, "That is an incredible power you've got there. Keeping us thinking that we were walking when in fact we were not moving. Are you some kind of magician?"

The guardian smiled. "Not at all, it is just a little display of my power." Answered Tnias Silativ, the guardian of the third tower. Hogin tower being the ignition point for all the water of Noom Live Kingdom, it was a highly strategic gate.

"I was just dedicating a few minutes to the proper mourning procedures before allowing you to come to your certain death. You see, the guardian you've just defeated was my brother from another mother, but my brother nonetheless and I was lighting a candle for his soul that it may depart in peace." He gestured affectionately toward the flickering candle.

"Unlike the people of Noom Live Kingdom that don't believe in anything, I *do* believe in something, and what I believe in the most at this moment is that you two are going down today."

His countenance darkened and his power rose immensely.

• • • • • •• • ••

"There was a man, quite a prestigious man who resided in the court; he was a lady's man, but he had his family and a loving wife despite this. A boy was born and he was proud of his boy, but he thought to himself that it was better to have many more for a long and lasting dynasty; unluckily for him, all his attempts were a failures and his wife only bore a single boy, and ten girls as they tried to conceive another.

One day he was feeling down and went to one of his mistresses. When his mistress saw that he was so blue, she inquired about his unhappiness. He then explained to her his situation in full detail, of how he tried and tried with no luck, and that he would give anything to have another boy. In that moment, the mistress promised him to give him and son and made him happy that day.

Nine months later, he had a son and it was named Sutama. Unfortunately, the mother of the boy had complications on delivering the baby. The baby was so strong and did not want to be born. It cost her her very life to bring Sutama into the world. His father then took him to his house as one of his own, and it was not until the father was very old that that the boy, now a man, was informed of his true origin.

That man happened to be my father, and that boy happened to be my brother, the one you've just killed." Said Tnias Silativ. "It is my duty to honor him by defeating not only one of you, but both of you.

• • • • • • • ••

Tnias Silativ never wanted to become a fighter, much less a guardian. Stories say that he was training his young brother in the ways of fighting, and he only wanted to become a fighter for Soultai Tournament.

Tnias Silativ and his brother made a blood pact that he would endure until he was ready, and would only be fulfilled when Tnias Silativ would tell him so. In exchange, Tnias Silativ would train him in all types of weapons and fighting styles and join him in his quest to become the champion at the Soultai Tournament.

Legend says that when Tnias Silativ was fighting at the tournament, all of his matches were won by completely wiping out his opponents without the need to use any weapons at all. He carried his sword, but he never used it. His fighting style, informed by close hand-to-hand combat techniques, was one of a kind. In the first round, Tnias Silativ knocked his opponent out with one punch, and with his second punch he crashed his head into the ground.

During the second round, he kicked his opponent, cracking his ribs and entirely dislocating one of his legs. With the second kick, a cracking sound emanated from the neck of the opponent...indicating sudden death.

The third round only lasted less than two minutes; he jumped onto his opponent and with a shime-waza choke combined with the rear naked choke, triangle chokes, and gi chokes, he killed his opponent.

In the fourth and final round, he introduced his kickboxing techniques, which were specially designed to destroy the chest, lungs and heart of an opponent. It was a display of pure brute force, combined with ancient martial arts technique, that of the gods, so they say.

Tnias Silativ wanted to go for the Champion of Champions title, but that happened to be gained by his brother. But before challenging the champion, King Rosuled approaching him to test his strength. The legend says that he fought one round with King Rosuled and proved himself to be worthy of the Tnias title.

Chapter 20

"The might and power of this man is so strong, he is even surpassing my strength. No, he has *already* surpassed my strength! That is why I will rely on him in all my battles; I don't have to fight much and he gets to fight the strongest opponent in the Kingdom. But I have been observing him lately and there is something changing inside of him. He is my pupil and I have taught him everything he knows, but my brother is starting to develop a hunger for power.

Every time we get into a battle, I can see him craving and longing for the strongest enemy. His reputation and his power have grown exponentially, so much so that he is even more popular than I in the Kingdom. I can have others more popular than me, I don't mind, because they will never surpass me or usurp my Kingdom.

The story with my brother is different, however. That is the reason why I always ask him to wear his armor, because I don't want others to see his face in battle. Nobody knows and nobody *will* know that we are brothers, but he is so powerful that I cannot any longer have him by my side. He is the only threat to my crown and Kingdom.

I will ask him to fight the last battle for me, but he is no longer my pupil, there is nothing else I can teach him. After this battle I must get rid of him, but I must be careful because he is indeed stronger than I." These were the reflections of King Rosuled, one dreary and rainy afternoon spent atop the highest tower in his castle.

Years passed and the jealousy of the King grew, until one day he came up with a brilliant plan.

"Brother, you will start your own quests, it is time for you to make your own name known! After all, nobody knows of our relationship. Go! Go and find the strongest warrior in the land, and if you meet with defeat, that is your punishment, but I don't think a warrior capable of defeating you exists. There is a very rich and special plot of land that I will grant to you, here you can create your Kingdom after all your years of battles and fighting." Said the King to his brother.

"I only have very few conditions for you. You will always be ready when I call you to battle; you will pledge to abide by my rule; and, most of all, no matter how powerful or wise you become, you will never fight me, for I am your master. These are my conditions." Proclaimed the King. "One more thing. You will take my one and only child with you and raise him as your own. Moreover, you are never to tell him his true identity; when the time comes, I will have a place for him in my Kingdom as my son. No one knows this but you, his mother died while giving birth and I am entrusting this child to you, as you have just lost yours a few short hours ago."

"It is my pleasure to serve you, I will gladly accept your terms and I will always keep your conditions in my heart. You are my only brother, my master and my everything. I will honor you in everything that I do!" Said the brother. "But I would like to fight by your side one last time." He concluded. The two brothers went and fought their last battle together, after which Kind Rosuled remained within his Kingdom and his brother went to establish his own Kingdom in the territory given to him by his lovely brother.

Many years later, King Rosuled wanted to test the loyalty of his brother, and so called him to accompany him on a holy quest.

He sent a messenger with the following words:

"Brother, I want you to accompany me to this battle, we are going to wipe out a rebel group. In fact, we are going on a holy crusade to purge the soil for those called the "*Snaitsirch*," but I don't want anyone to see your face. You shall wear your armor as you have done in the past. I want to see the man everybody has spoken of in the legends of my Kingdom; I want to see that warrior in action, I want to see the *Unspeakable Warrior* by my side once more."

. . . .

"I must say, I am impressed with your power. The ones I saw fighting for the other Kingdom were strong and powerful, but nothing compared to you two." Said Tnias Silativ. "It is so unfortunate to waste two such great warriors like yourselves for the sake of who knows what." He continued saying.

"Why are you in my dominion and what are you looking for?" He Asked.

"Sadly for you we don't have time to talk to the likes of you." Replied Lightning Sword, placing his hand upon the hilt of his sword. "Let me tell you how this is going to happen. My partner here, The Emissary, will head to the next tower and I will fight you here. There is no need for you to worry about anything, we just don't have time to waste with you. After all, your defeat is inevitable so why prolong it any longer than is necessary?"

When the Emissary moved to pass to the next tower, Tnias Silativ threw his first blow, and it was so powerful that the wind churned up into a tornado around them. But Lightning Sword blocked the blow with his bare hands, strangling the very air with raw strength.

"As I said before, my partner is going to the next tower and you are going down." He released the tornado upon the guardian and struck him with thunderous force.

"I see, I thought the strong one was the old one, but it looks like you are strong as well. I will agree to your request and let him pass. I would love to fight you and see your strength." Said the guardian as he recovered himself.

"Now *that* is what I am talking about! Have a great fight and don't take too long." Laughed the Emissary. "Lightning Sword, I am heading to meet next guardian."

· · · · · · · ··

Hont Well is the cradle of civilization and holds the most terrifying secrets of all time. Its King, Rosuled, is the very personification of deceit and lies. He is the most wise and cunning of all the kings.

He created a secret chamber containing the most powerful attributes that he stole from humankind. There are six relics hiding inside of Hont Well's walls. Three of the Fruit and three of the Gifts group. These powerful weapons belong to humanity, and their power can be held only by humans. These Kingdoms enjoy only the shadows of these powers.

Hont well has been keeping the Gift of Prophecy, keeping humanity from receiving the True message of God Almighty, delivering lies to humanity instead. As King Rosuled also holds the "Gift of Wisdom" and the "Gift of Knowledge" in his chamber, he is able to mislead human kind with these powerful talents held captive since ancient times. But being able to manipulate humanity through his deceitful methods and cunning has not satisfied him.

Hont Well, or, more specifically, King Rosuled, has been holding three elements of the Fruit of the Spirit from humanity; these are "*Love, Joy, and Peace.*"

It is said that humanity has lost its love and joy, and the only path left to them is war, which is the opposite of peace; building nuclear weapons, lethal viruses undetected by human eyes and so much more. What humanity does not know is that all of these are caused by the spiritual forces at Hont Well Kingdom and by its King.

King Rosuled can only influence and use others for his atrocious acts against humanity, he cannot directly influence humans. King Rosuled hates humanity the most because they are the only creatures in the universe who are able to hold and unleash the true power of these Holy Relics.

He is in a search of a far greater treasure, and he has been waiting for ages for the right human to show him the way. *That* is his secret plot, the one no one knows. King Rosuled is in search of the "*Tree of Life*" in "*Nede Land's Garden.*" Ancient scrolls and books speak about it and place the location somewhere in Hont Well Kingdom, but it can only be found by a worthy human. King Rosuled has tried for ages to find it with no success at all. He is just waiting for the right one to entice and deceive.

Chapter 21

"Let us not waste any time." Said Lightning Sword, formerly known as Kimura Ichi. He immediately charged the guardian with full strength, landing right on his face. This initiated a dizzying flurry of combinations that struck the guardian all over his body. He did not notice that Tnias Silativ was not even defending himself. And suddenly, Tnias Silativ threw his first blow, thrashing Lightning Sword to the ground. He was able to stand up quickly, but the guardian countered his maneuver and threw him back to the ground. Every time there was a blow from Tnias Silativ, Lightning Sword ate dust and was struck down.

"How many times are you going to get up? You know, you are no match for me, I am just toying with you! I am not even using my real power. I just wanted you to feel my anger." Said Tnias Silativ in a mocking tone.

"Well," Lightning Sword began, regaining his composure, "I will get up as many times as is needed to defeat you, until I defeat you and meet my partner at the next tower."

"Oh boy! Since you don't plan on giving up, I will end this now!" He hit Lightning Sword savagely, so hard, in fact, the guardian himself believed he'd gone a bit overboard.

Yet, with what appeared to be no effort at all, Lightning Sword managed to get on his feet once again. "Is it my body moving by itself, I don't feel anything…" Like an animated corpse, he charged the guardian with increased strength and tenacity.

"Where is *this* power coming from? You are almost dead and you insist on continuing!" The guardian thrashed him and threw him to the ground, stepping on his face afterward.

"Die once and for all, mortal."

The battle was over, thought the guardian, turning to leave.

"Matte Kudasai," whispered Lightning Sword in Japanese, which means "wait please."

"The battle is not over…" This time, Lighting Sword stood bolt straight in front of the guardian in full armor. A golden helmet, diamond shield, bronze breastplate, silver belt and Spartan sandals wreathed with fire and electrical arcs. His sword was also lit with flames and crawling with lightning energy. Stepping forward little by little, as someone who can barely walk, he inched closer to the guardian ominously.

"Ha! I see!" Said the guardian. "You were concealing your true power from me. You seem to have a death wish. Since you have unsheathed your sword, I will grant you a quick death as response."

"No one has ever seen my sword and live. In fact, I have never used it because none of my previous opponents were up to your level. I see now that you are a worthy opponent, but as I said before, it is a shame that you have to die." The guardian whispered, menacingly.

"Die now!" Unleashing his secret sword technique, the guardian rushed his enemy and went for the quick kill. But this time, Lightning Sword moved too fast, and issuing bolts of lightning in every direction that shook the gate and the very ground itself, the guardian could not keep up with the speed, and Lightning Sword landed a blow that stroke the guardian's leg.

"I finally understand the power behind the armor. It is so powerful, but somehow its power is not yet fully awake, there is something I am missing, and my sword is craving something that I am unaware of." Lightning Sword thought to himself.

"I will play with you a little bit more, at least until I understand this new power. Don't you die on me too quick, guardian! Try to keep up!" The clashing of swords were mistaken as a ferocious storm by the citizens of the nearby hills, so deafening and incredible was the power emanating from these two warriors. Lightning Sword fell upon the ground, his armor lying on the ground next to him in pieces. And like dust, his armor vanished into thin air.

"I see that your armor has rejected you. With it, you could have defeated me, but without your armor, you will never defeat me! You are once again a pathetic fighter, so I will bring peace to your sword." Said the guardian, and unleashed his most powerful sword attack against Lightning Sword.

A bright flash issued from out of nowhere. "What happened? I could not see anything." He was badly wounded, and he was truck dumb with disbelief.

"Don't worry, and don't try to understand what just happened. Allow me to indulge you and enlighten you."

"Yes…" The guardian whispered as blood gurgled from his mouth.

"The armor did not reject me. I discovered its true power; the armor became my body and I became the armor. There was no need for externalities any longer, they were just a place holder, but yet my sword is not complete. Something is missing…" Concluded Lightning Sword reflectively.

"Thank you for being the one to allow me to fully comprehend my strength and discover the true potential behind the armor."

"You...you are welcome." A strange smile crept across the guardians face as he said this, and he expired.

Looking down at his fist, Lightning Sword said, "There is something powerful within me and I must share it with the Emissary. He must understand the true meaning of the armor to become even stronger. I will hurry to him now."

. . . .

"I am Tnias Nabla, and I can see that I am the only one left standing. All the other Tnias have been defeated by you or your partner. Just a few seconds ago I felt the life of Tnias Silativ fade away and I cannot sense it anymore. I don't claim to be the strongest of the four of us, but I will honor my post, no one is to pass."

"Sorry, no time to talk." said the Emissary, charging full bore against the guardian. But the guardian parried the attack without even blinking. "I said that I do not claim to be the strongest *myself*, but others do. Whatever luck you've had before, it runs out here. Your pathetic attack won't touch me."

"If that is the case, let me show you some of my real power." Said the Emissary, transforming into his full-fledged Knightly form.

"Charging again against the guardian, the Emissary used a powerful technique that would have felled anyone else, but the guardian did not move. "What is going on, why I am not able to reach him? I can feel my armor craving something as well. It is trying to tell me something, but I cannot understand it." Thought the Emissary as he charged once again against his enemy. But this time, the guardian moved to the side and blocked the attack.

"Well, it looks like I *can* reach you after all." Laughed the Emissary. "I think I have found my answer now." He continued, and at that moment, the guardian threw his first blow, sending the Emissary to the ground, badly injured. "As I said before, your pathetic attacks cannot reach me." The guardian stepped forward and examined the Emissary carefully.

"I should end you know for all your transgressions and your insolence." He sneered with contempt, clenching his fist. Tnias Nabla made up his mind and went for a killing blow, but astonishingly he met Lightning Sword mid-air, who deflected his strike and turned him away for the moment.

"I am not too late, Am I?" Inquired Lightning Sword.

"Well," the Emissary spat while rising to his feet with some effort, "I am having a little trouble with this one, but it is always a good time to help a friend when in need." He concluded, taking Lightning Swords hand.

"You need to understand the real power behind your armor."

"Wait! Are you telling me you already received your armor?" Inquired the Emissary.

"Yes, I have, but I have also discovered the real power behind it and its true potential. I hurried here to tell you about, but I did not know you were being thrashed. It looks like this one is not like the others." He said as he looked over to the guardian who, having recovered, was staring back at them.

"Allow me to repay the kindness you have shown to my partner." Said Lightning Sword before striking back at Tnias Nabla, forcing him to block the attack. Meanwhile, the Emissary took to one knee, still winded from the battle.

"Wait! Wait a minute! I am his opponent, do not interfere!" Shouted the Emissary. "I did not want to show my real power, but I guess I have no other option." He rose once more to his feet.

At that moment, the armor of the Emissary vanished completely, revealing a great warrior who now shone a flaming number zero on his chest, blazing through his shirt.

"You see, our ranks and strength are measured from ten to one. One being the strongest of all of us; however, my power is that of the zero, the greatest of them all, which I have always tried to conceal, but you are a worthy opponent. You've trashed the ground with me while I was in my previous state, so let us see how you handle this level." Said the Emissary, inquisitively.

"I see! You knew the real power behind the armor and how to use it all along." Exclaimed Lightning Sword.

"Of course I did. I am the one who trained all the members of the squad and I was a warrior long before all of this started. I was just waiting for the Lord to show me the way and put on my path those who could learn and use His power for good. I am impressed that you are moving at such a great speed with your transformations. I see why The Lord God Almighty chose you. Even though I have not trained you, you have mastered the real power of the armor. The secret is one to be discovered by each warrior and it cannot be passed from one to other. But you have mastered it indeed. Now, allow me to show you the real power we possess and where it comes from!" The Emissary now pointed his mighty sword at the guardian.

In a flash the Emissary unleashed a blinding array of attacks, all of which the guardian deflected, but with great effort. One of the last two strikes hit him in the chest, and caused him to bleed.

"I have not seen my blood in ages. Only King Rosuled himself has made me bleed. *You* are the second one." Said Tnias Nabla, gleefully.

"I can see that you are strong and with the information you just gave me I can deduce that your kind is stronger than all. No wonder we were the ones sent to this Kingdom. Your strength could not be met by any of my other partners." Remarked the Emissary.

The guardian smiled and lunged with full strength against the Emissary, throwing him on the ground as before. But now, the Emissary immediately rebounded and countered with a blow that plunged into the guardian's stomach. Blood gushed from his mouth.

"You cocky human, you think because you did this…" he held up his hand with blood dripping from it, "you can defeat me!? Take this!" Shouted Tnias Nabla, enraged and clearly more hurt than he let on. Like a trapped animal, the guardian lashed out at the Emissary, who was now bleeding.

"Are you sure you don't need any help? I would like to fight this strong dude myself if you're done with him!" Yelled Lightning Sword.

"It is time to finish the fight." Called back the Emissary as he summoned his secret technique which was now more powerful than ever. The Emissary spoke the mighty words, "Heavenly Sword" and with a display of indescribable power, sublime and radiant swords descended from the sky in a rain of heavenly light. The guardian…was no more. The greatest and last of the Tnias Order was defeated, as was the last of the Towers.

The two warriors were now ready to head to the main hall and enter the Kingdom.

Chapter 22

Word came to King Rosuled...

"Your sanctity, the four towers have fallen, and the intruders are now entering the main hall of Hont Well. Should I summon Lebezej and Laab to finish them?" Inquired Tseirp.

"You will do no such thing. There is no need for them to come. If they meet with them by accident, it is well, but I will not have them fight the intruders. Let them come to me. I will take care of them on my own. I will summon the guardians of my secret treasure."

"But, your sanctity, you have never summoned them. We don't even know who they are."

"Are you questioning me?"

"No, no my liege."

"Good. There is no need for you to know them, when the time comes, if it must come to that, I will summon them and you will then learn of them. In the meantime, let them come to me."

Tseirp hesitated, but decided to hazard the comment. "You can summon the *Unspeakable Warrior*, your highness. He has proven to be the most fearsome in our lands and the people are talking already about the guardians of the towers and the defeat they suffered."

The King turned to face Tseirp. "I will let you know in due time." Said King Rosuled, staring deeply into Tseirp's eyes, unflinchingly. "You are dismissed."

"The intruders are now in the hall and they have engaged the guards." Said Tseirp.

"Attention all guards! No one is to fight the two warriors, lead them to me instead!" Commanded the King. "I think it is time for me to summon my guardians."

Using his secret chamber, the King summoned the two guardians of the treasure.

Now, standing in front of the King was the Unspeakable Warrior and the second guardian of the secret treasure, but there was a third being that came to heed the call. "Why is he here? Why did you bring your peasant boy to my Kingdom?"

Inquired the King of the Unspeakable Warrior, angrily.

"I allowed you to get away with him from the battlefield and now you are bringing him to my Kingdom?" The King was incensed.

"But my King, he is the guardian of the door on earth and he is the only one that could transport us here to answer the call. Without him, it would have taken us weeks to get here."

• • • • • • • • • • • •••

The mere presence of a descendant of the Snaitsirch group was an abomination to King Rosuled. Years ago, when the Unspeakable Warrior took away a peasant boy and raised him as his own, he did not say anything because he thought he would never see him again in his life.

Now, having the presence of this warrior in his face was a bigger threat to this Kingdom than the two approaching warriors.

"Is my brother teasing me or tempting me? I cannot fight him, he knows that, and that is why he brought the peasant warrior with him." The King thought to himself.

"He is the embodiment of deception and denial, he is the descendant of those that could really harm my Kingdom and now my brother, the Unspeakable Warrior, has brought him to me. I shall wait for the correct opportunity, but I must place enmity and division among them; after all, I am the master of deception and war." Thought King Rosuled.

The Unspeakable Warrior knew all the details, but his two companions did not know what was happening.

When the mighty King Babul Ell asked Larey, the guardian of the gate to earth to bring him and Ell, his son, to Hont Well, he did not know what to expect. It was a complete surprise, but he is the King.

"I don't understand why we have come to the capital, father." Said Ell to his father, King Babul Ell. At this moment, a great truth was about to be revealed.

"Welcome, my brother, the Unspeakable Warrior!" Shouted King Rosuled, setting his evil plan in motion.

"Wait! Brother, father! What is happening! Why is the King of Hont Well calling you "brother" and the "Unspeakable Warrior?" Asked Ell, candidly.

"Is this your son, Ell? Come closer, my son, allow me to light your mind and feed your soul today." The King took the boy's head in his hands gingerly, and looked into his eyes with apparent kindness.

"The mighty Babul Ell is my brother, and I am his master, trainer and King. Not only that, but I am glad to see my dear son. I see you have the eyes and the charm of your mother, it is a shame that she passed away and could not see this day." Continued King Rosuled.

Your majesty, out of respect, but I don't understand what you are talking about. My father is your brother and the King of Hont Well is my uncle. Is that what you are trying to tell me? No, I am your uncle, said King Babul Ell, your real father is King Rosuled.

"We made a pact a long time ago and you were part of that pact. *I* was to raise you as my son and train you my way, to get you ready for my brother to call upon us and reveal to you the truth. I swear I tried to tell you many times, but I did not have the heart and I could not betray the pact I made with my brother, whom I loved unconditionally." Explained King Babul Ell.

"Why are you the Unspeakable Warrior?" Ell asked sheepishly.

"We will deal with this on another occasion." Said King Rosuled, cheerfully. It was not yet time to reveal the details of the naked truth.

"I need you to deal with these two intruders that have come to my Kingdom." The King waved his hand casually. "They have already defeated the guardians of my towers, including the guardian for Babul Ell Kingdom. They are very strong, and I have summoned you to honor your pact and finish them." Said King Rosuled, suddenly quite serious.

When Larey heard these words, he knew something was wrong and something evil was about to happen, but he did not know what it could be.

"These are the companions of the ones I trained; they must be strong if they are able to get to the capital by themselves." Thought Larey. "I will watch and see how powerful they are."

At this moment, the Emissary and Lightning sword were coming in, escorted by all the guards of the palace.

"You are not welcome here!" King Rosuled boomed. "You have defeated my guardians, showing your strength and power, but here stand the strongest beings in all Nede Land, and the second Strongest, who happens to be my son. I am sure they are the ones who defeated your friends at Babul Ell Kingdom, since he is the almighty King Babul Ell."

When Babul Ell heard this, he said to his son Ell, or nephew, "This is not the time to sob or lament. We will speak later but deal with *them* now."

"But father, why? Why, why?"

"It is okay, Ell, you will always be my son, no matter what happened in the past." He said with a smile.

When the almighty King Babul Ell was about to start the fight, Larey interrupted and said, "Your highness, my King, these two are not worthy of your sword, allow Ell and myself to deal with them."

Chapter 23

The Kingdom was now in an awful commotion, eager to know what the King would do with the intruders, but they wouldn't dare speak up. King Rosuled is the most patient King, but at the same time, the least tolerant of interruptions.

"I can sense the armor within me yearning for something in this Kingdom; there is something calling from within my heart, and from within my spirit," thought Lightning Sword, "but I don't know what it is."

"Alright, I am Ell the mighty."

"And I am Larey, the peasant warrior." He said. Upon hearing these words, King Rosuled felt annoyed and angry, but it was not yet time.

"Why do they call you the peasant warrior?" Inquired the Emissary.

"I still don't know, but I am sure I will figure it out someday. It might be because I am indeed a peasant, or because someone made up a nick name from me that fir, but there is no need to worry about it."

"I can see you are stronger than your friends and I am very glad to be here to experience the display of power. Sadly for you, you will not see it for long." Said Larey in response.

"Your sanctity, do you think it is a good idea to let the stranger, the peasant boy, handle this issue? There are rumors in all Nede Land about this warrior and his deeds. If he decides to turn against us, we will be in a real predicament." Whispered the King's Advisor, Tseirp.

"In that case, let us fight one on one. I have tested the strength of your partner, Judge and he was a formidable opponent." Said Ell. "I am very glad to cross your path, as I was told there was someone stronger than Judge and I felt the irresistible need to drive a sword into that person. I never thought that the day would come so soon, though."

"I have seen the power of Judge and Discerner evolving as they fight. They've even reached their maximum level of strength, and thanks to that, they are still alive and heading back to earth." Remarked Larey.

"Thank you much for the information and the comforting news. For a minute I thought that they had perished, but you are telling me that they made it out alive and well. That is all I could have asked for." Said the Emissary in relief.

"I will be your opponent." He said to Larey.

"And *I* will be *your* opponent." Said Lightning Sword to Ell, pointing his sword at him with a grin.

"Before you two die, what are your names?" Asked Larey.

"I don't think we will be the ones dying, but I am called the Emissary." He said with a bow.

"And I am called Lightning Sword."

"Since this is the real deal, let us not waste time with children's games. We will not insult you by using poor displays of power!" At that moment, the two warriors stood side by side, both displaying the number zero on their chests, flames coming from their feet and emanating a great heat from their bodies.

The fight was one for the immortals, as they fought like gods of old. The clash was spectacular and overwhelming. The whole palace shook and all within it trembled.

The Emissary opened with his heavenly sword technique, but he did not know who he was facing. Larey blocked or dodged all the falling swords with great skill and agility, enabling him to land the first blow while the Emissary was recovering from the attack. Though it was a superficial cut, and nothing to worry about, the Emissary increased his strength to its maximum, and was able to send Larey tumbling backward close to King Rosuled.

Lightning Sword was caught up in the strike from Larey as well.

"They are really strong, I am using my maximum strength but they keep coming and we are not getting anywhere." Said the Emissary.

"I share that sentiment with you. We need to find a way to defeat them, I did not come to this world to lose in my first crusade, fighting for The Lord God Almighty. Something is hungering within me and I can feel it; it is like there is a *Hero Within* me," said Lightning Sword, "but I cannot understand it very well."

"You two deserves all the credit for defeating the guardians, you are really strong. Your partner, Judge, had almost the same power level as you, but somehow you are stronger than him. However, that will not be enough to defeat either of us." Said Ell.

"I decided to call the fight with him a truce, because he was the first one in a long time to make me sweat and bleed and the only one to break my sword. He deserved it. Now, you two must show that you want to live if you want to get out of here alive!" Shouted Larey.

"I did not say they could leave alive from this place!" Bellowed the King. "In fact, I clearly stated that I wanted them terminated! How dare you defy me!" Larey only looked at him with an evil vengeance burning in his eyes.

"Stand up and fight!" Yelled Larey. "Stop concealing your power, you are just like Judge and Discerner, always concealing your real power. Don't you see that you will die if you don't reveal your true power!"

"Is he with us or *against* us?" Though both the Emissary and Lightning Sword. "It looks somehow like he is sympathizing with us. Let us grant his wish and release our true potential."

When the two warriors displayed their incredible power, it was unbelievable.

Their opponents could not see where the power was coming from, but it was a devastating power that then exploded directly at Ell and Larey. The powerful strikes were indeed devastating, but their swords were met in the air every single time, deflected. The Emissary and Lightning Sword fell down, seemingly defeated.

"Ah! I know you two are not dead! Stand up and fight!" Larey screamed. That is when Ell told him, "Why are you encouraging them?" "Did you want the fight of your life or not? Were you looking for great warriors who could stand against you or not, huh?" Asked Larey, turning to face Ell with a furious look in his eyes. "There they are!" He flung his arm in the direction of the two warriors with conviction. "Fight them and get the satisfaction you have always yearned for."

They leapt onto the motionless bodies the Emissary and Lightning Sword, and the fight appeared to be over. The two heroes were both like corpses on the ground, bleeding profusely.

"They were strong, they made me sweat. They were worthy opponents." Said Ell.

"Peasant boy, go and make sure they are dead." Shouted King Rosuled.

"I am not a boy…" Mumbled Larey as he walked over to them to make sure they were dead. Suddenly, the apparently dead warriors rose from the ground and stood erect.

"*The Hero Within* is calling and they are to come…" Both warriors said in an otherworldly pair of voices.

No one was able to understand what they were saying.

"They are hallucinating!" They all thought as they watched them fall on the ground again, motionless.

"The fight is not over…" Coming from within the walls, a mighty sword appeared, radiating a great light that was reflected in both hands of each warrior. Now holding four glorious swords, the

Emissary and Lightning Sword stood once more, the one holding the "*Sword of Prophecy*" and the "*Sword of Wisdom*" and the other holding the "*Sword of Knowledge*" and the "*Sword of Joy.*"

The cry they were feeling from within was the cry of the Gifts and the Fruit of the Spirit calling out to them. These are the most powerful weapons that only humanity can hold.

Both warriors, seemingly moving with a fluidity and effortlessness that defied understanding, let loose on Larey and Ell with unimaginable power, forcing them to start blocking the attacks.

Something unexpected happened and the two swords the Emissary was holding merged and became one.

"Awesome!" Exclaimed the Emissary, conscious again and freely moving. The same thing happened to Lightning Sword's weapons, as he was now holding an altogether different sword.

"What power," thought Larey, "I did not know that the Sword would take on a life of its own to save these warriors."

Larey was still thinking when he saw two more swords breaking through the walls of the castle with a shattering sound. It was the "*Sword of Love*" and it went right for the Emissary's hand, while the "*Sword of Peace*" went hurtling toward Lightning Sword's hand.

"I cannot believe this is happening! That is not possible! How can the Swords break through and escape from their prison? They must not get back to earth, or else the salvation of humanity would be accomplished!" King Rosuled exclaimed in his mind with fury and confusion. "I knew the Swords were powerful, but I did not know they could think for themselves. But they are not really what I want, thought King Rosuled, calming himself. "I want the ultimate power of them all and I will get it no matter what. After all, I cannot clasp them. They are useless to me and they can only be used by a human, but I did not want humanity to regain these powers."

Then the King shouted out loud, "Kill them before they get stronger, you pathetic sack! You petulant peasant boy, if you would have done what I told you in the first place, none of this would have happened. They are getting stronger because of your arrogance!"

No one could understand why the King was so angry with Larey.

"Brother! Calm down or you're going to have a stroke." Said King Babul Ell.

"What! Am I a human now? To have strokes?" Asked the King, angrier.

"Don't you know the true identity of the peasant boy? Do you know that the Unspeakable Warrior of all the legends in Hont Well Kingdom is none other than my brother, the almighty King Babul Ell! And when we went to annihilate your whole wretched family, you were one of them, peasant boy. The almighty King Babul Ell *is* that warrior! And on that day he picked you up from the rubbish, but not before slaughtering all your family and bringing them to ashes." The King revealed his true intentions now.

"Father, what is he talking about?" Inquired Ell, still calling King Babul Ell his father.

That is when King Babul Ell shared the story with them all. How he picked up Larey from the peasant family and raised him to be one of the greatest warriors of all time.

"I do not regret my actions, I am proud of you, Larey." Said King Babul Ell, placing his hand on Larey.

"You...you mean that you butchered my family and took me with you? I cannot believe these words! This man must be lying."

"I don't lie, boy, you are suffering from brain damage or memory loss, that you cannot accept the reality."

Ell continued fighting with his opponent, still hurting them viciously. Lightning Sword was now bleeding more than ever, and on the other hand, Larey, out of anger after hearing these words, unleashed his fury against the Emissary.

"I was trying to save you and your precious earth from destruction, but my anger is too much to control now! I must end you and find out the truth behind these hideous accusations."

Ell could not believe the day they were having either, it was as if their entire lives were reduced to this moment and they were both in complete denial. Mostly Larey, who cared so much for his foster father that he could not even lay a finger on his King.

Larey then decided to train two human warriors because he said that he would never lay a finger on his father, but the pain was so immeasurable, so intense, that he could not believe them. He wanted to destroy these thoughts and forget his promise. His thoughts were resonating with pure fury, impregnated now, not only in his mind, but in his heart, with malice.

When clashing swords, the newly combined Sword of the Emissary, containing the Gifts and the Fruit of the Spirit, hit Larey and cut his forehead, dazing him.

At this moment, Larey started to remember his boyhood. His father told him a story he could not remember perfectly, but he saw the happiness his father and mother brought to him. His father was hugging him and kissing him; he was playing with his sisters and having fun, then darkness came upon his vision.

He saw this great army attacking their family and killing them one by one. He saw his parents being killed by an Unspeakable Warrior. Larey was not able to remember that the man perpetrating these atrocious acts is the same man that took him when he was a child, the same man that raised him as his son. The man he called "father," killed his family…and that man is King Babul Ell.

Larey was now turned to face King Babul Ell. He wanted to hear from his lips that these words were not true, even though he'd seemingly recovered his memory, he was in shock and disbelief.

"Tell me it's a lie." Meanwhile, the fight had not stopped, Larey was lost in this thoughts and Ell could not believe all these cunning accusations. Lightning Sword and the Emissary were feeling nothing but pain and sorrow for this poor and hurt soul called Larey.

"Tell me, please tell me that all of this is not true!" Screamed Ell, asking for clear explanations from his father, or uncle, King Babul Ell. At this moment, the mighty Babul Ell confessed his crimes in a sign of pride for his adopted son, saying, "Yes, it is all true. That was one of best and worst days in my life. I was suffering from the loss of my child and on that day, I saw courage in you and I thought you could be my son." Now facing Larey.

"Can you ever forgive me, my Larey?" Asked the almighty King Babul Ell.

"You have confessed your crimes and you are asking for forgiveness. But I don't see a *shred* of repentance in you. I don't think I can ever forgive you."

"You insolent boy," shouted Babul Ell, "I made you who you are. You would be dead if it was not for me. You were destined to die that day along with your family, but I spared you and you dare to confront me! What are you going to do about it, boy?" Asked King Babul Ell, angrily.

"I tried to forget when you went to earth and killed the love of my life. You also tried to kill my son. Yes, you tried to kill him, but he is very much alive."

"You are lying, I received reports from my most trusted sources that your child died." The King was shocked.

"Yes, I'm sure you did. But I fabricated these reports and made certain you received them because I knew you would never ceased to chase my son otherwise. You killed his mother; you killed the woman I loved."

"*You* were not supposed to mingle with humans," King Babul Ell stepped forward, enraged, "and you fell for a filthy woman! On top of that, you procreated a child with her. That was an abomination and I had to put an end to it!

"You cruel bastard! You have killed everything precious in my life; you killed my family, you killed my parents, you killed the one I loved and you tried to kill my only son! You will pay for this!" Larey shouted in contempt and anger that boiled over.

"It was not my crusade, it was not my calling, it was King Rosuled's holy crusade that was meant wipe out that town and all its people." Replied King Babul Ell.

"Yes, it was. I understand it now, but you were the sword that pierced my family. I blame him for all of this, but I blame you more! You are really unspeakable and diabolic, the most cunning of you all." Replied Larey, now in battle position, ready to attack King Babul Ell. When he sent the first blow against King Babul Ell, his son Ell blocked the attack.

"I did not see that coming. Instead of fighting with us, they are fighting among themselves. We have the swords, so let us go." The Emissary said to Lightning Sword.

And in that moment, King Rosuled stepped down from his throne to stand side by side with his brother, and side by side with his newly found son, Ell. Across from them, there was Larey, the Emissary, and Lightning Sword, all ready for the battle. A three on three.

"You are not the chosen ones and you are *not* yet ready to fight them." Said Larey. The almighty Babul Ell threw his first attack to kill both the Emissary and Lighting Sword, they were not able to dodge the attack and were severely injured.

When Larey saw this, he jumped and grabbed the Emissary and Lightning Sword to transport them back to earth. He was the only one able to transport others and move them between Kingdoms.

"Larey has betrayed the King and all of Nede Land, he is now an outlaw. Anyone who sees him must attempt to bring him to me, dead or alive." This was the command of King Rosuled.

Larey was able to say a few words before taking his two new friends back to earth.

"*I will see you again, and when I come, all Nede Land will tremble before me.*"

Dear Reader,

I hope you enjoyed the first books in the series: *The Hero Within: Awareness, Power, Nede Land 1 & Nede Land 2*

I have to tell you, I really love this hero story. Many readers wrote me asking, "What's next for our Hero?" Well, be sure to stay tuned because the saga of publishing Christian Fiction isn't quite over. Our Hero will be back in book four. Will he have more power? I sure hope so.

When I wrote *The Hero Within: Nede Land 3;* I got many letters from fans thanking me for the books. Some had opinions about the adventures, while others simply rooted for Babul Ell.

As an author, I love feedback. Candidly, you're the reason I will explore the Hero's future. So tell me what you liked, what you loved, even what you hated. You can write to me at comments@christianhero.org and visit me on the web at www.christianhero.org.

Finally, I need to ask a favor. If you're so inclined, I'd love a review of *The Hero Within: Nede Land 3.* Loved it, hated it—I'd just enjoy your feedback.

Reviews can be tough to come by these days, and you, the reader, have the power to make or break a book. If you have the time, *here's a link to my author page, along with all my books on Amazon: http://amzn.to/19p3dNx*

Thank you so much for reading *The Hero Within: Nede Land 3* and for spending time with me.

In gratitude,

Yeral E. Ogando

Yeral E. Ogando comes from a very humble origin and continues to be a humble servant of our Lord Almighty; understanding that we are nothing but vessels and the Lord who called us, also sends us to do His work, not our work. *Luke 17:10 "So likewise ye, when ye shall have done all those things which are commanded you, say, We are unprofitable servants: we have done that which was our duty to do."*

Mr. Ogando was born in the Caribbean, Dominican Republic. He is the beloved father of two beautiful girls "Yeiris & Tiffany" and three handsome boys "Bennett, Ethan & Nathan"

Jesus brought him to His feet at the age of 16-17. Since then, he has served as Co-pastor, pastor, Bible School teacher, youth counselor, and church planter.

Fluent in several languages Mr. Ogando is the Creator and owner of an Online Translation Ministry operating since 2007; with Native Christian translators in more than 25 countries and translating into more than 250 languages.

(www.christian-translation.com),

The most exciting thing about his Translation Ministry is that thousands of people are receiving the Word of God in their native language on a daily basis and hundreds of ministries are able to reach the world through the work of Christian-Translation.com along with his network of websites in different languages related to Christian Translation and Christian Services.

Nede Land

He's earned several degrees among them: Master of Arts in Theological Studies, Master of Arts in Languages and Linguistics and Doctor of Philosophy in Theology.